EMPIRE
KATHY COOPMANS

Hannah

This is our Empire

Kathy Coopmans

Cover Model-BT Urruela and Tessi Conquest

Photographer-Eric Battershell

Cover Designer- Sommer Stein of Perfect Pear Creative

Editor: Julia Goda Editing Services

Formatting: CP Smith Affordable Formatting

DEDICATION

This book is for those who sacrifice.

PROLOGUE

I often wonder to myself as I sit here next to my husband, Cain, and our four-year-old daughter, Justice, what the future holds for our family now. It's been several years since I found out the truth about my parents and the secret lives they've led, about my father, John, being a hitman for my uncle Salvatore Diamond's Empire. At such a young age, my mother happened to be one too. That's how they met. One hitman to another. Kill after the kill. Blood after the blood. When I first found out my family was tied to the mafia, I thought I would never be able to forgive them for lying to me my entire life. My parents, the ones who loved me unconditionally, were cold-blooded killers. All I envisioned were all of the times my dad left for days, making me think he was gone on a business trip, when really, everything I owned came from the fact he killed people for a living. That the food we ate, the roof over our heads, my clothes they bought all came from the loss of someone's life. My head was a mess; my heart was broken until I met my uncle, who showed up unannounced and made me realize this was my destiny. My fate. Although he left me with the decision to choose. I chose this life. It is my life, my family's life, and in spite of the things we do, I would choose it all over again. EVERY. SINGLE. DAY. He could have ordered my family to return to New York years ago or never let them leave in the first place. He could have demanded my mom stand by his side, but he didn't. Instead, he let her go to protect me. To save my soul from the darkness that consumes us all.

It wasn't until my mother, Cecily Greer, found out she was pregnant with me that she decided it was time for her to step away from her duties as a Diamond to kill those who'd betrayed my family. My dad carried on to become one of the most notorious killers for the mafia. Kill after the kill. Blood after the blood. He chose to stay with the Diamond Empire. He also chose my freedom; to not expose his only child to the rancid smell of death, murder, and corruption.

I grew up as normal as the kids in my neighborhood did. Played with dolls and went on vacations, movies, and family outings. To the outside world, we were an ordinary American family. My mother was the lady on the block who devoted her life to her daughter and her nights to her family, cooking, cleaning and driving me back and forth to school. She even headed several fundraisers for the homeless. Because hey, the whole world knows the danger that lurks outside for the homeless, but never do people think the real danger lives next door.

To my real family, the ones whose same blood pumps through my veins, we were famous. The untouchables. Well, my parents were. I was oblivious. Blind and betrayed.

I remember asking my dad one time as we were cuddled on the couch, watching one of my princess movies for what had to have been the hundredth time to him, but to me, every time was the first. It was the classic Cinderella. Even though it was a movie about a wicked stepmother and the most beautiful princess I had ever seen. It was a movie that was special to my dad and me. It was our movie. I was his little princess. His sweetheart.

"Daddy," I had said.

"Yes, Princess." He looked down to me with those eyes that only a loving and protecting father has for his little girl; soft and tender, full of love. Those eyes always told me he would protect me from anyone or anything. Put me first before everybody else.

"What do you do when you leave home?" my innocent self-asked.

"I'm a consultant for a company called Diamond Enterprises. I help people fix their problems," he told me, then put his arm back around me and tugged my princess blanket tightly over us.

He didn't mean he fixed diamonds like the big one on my mom's finger or the ones in her ears he bought her. No, not my dad. I knew he meant huge problems. I had big math problems in school. I hated math. My teachers would always help me with them. Therefore, I thought my dad was a teacher. He helped big people fix big people problems. Little did I know he snuffed the life out of those so-called problems.

As I grew older, I never asked him about it again. I grew out of my princess movies, went straight into swimming, ice-skating, and having sleepovers. My childhood was perfect. My parents were attentive. Loving. I was adored.

And then, at sixteen years old, I met Cain. The forbidden boy to my family. That was the first time my dad forbade me anything. I couldn't understand what his vendetta against Cain's father had to do with him and me. To me, it was stupid, two teenage boys fighting over a girl way before I existed. My dad ended up being the lucky one who captured my mom's heart. So why couldn't he let it go? Let me enjoy my first love?

For two years, Cain and I snuck around, seeing one another behind my dad's back. We even eloped at eighteen. It was a nightmare, to say the least when my parents found out. They eventually forgave me. They had no choice, because my happiness was short-lived. My husband betrayed me too, just like them. He deceived me in the worst possible way. Again, always someone trying to protect me.

I close my eyes, trying to discard all the thoughts from my past. When I open them, it is to look over at my husband, who is now holding our daughter close to him like my dad used to do me. Things didn't start out as we both had hoped. My wedding day was ruined. It's one I will not live again. It's forgotten. Cain is forgiven.

We were apart for years after we got married. I've closed the doors to those years without him. Vowed to myself I would never open them again, and I haven't. I never will again. The love we share for one another and the miracle we created means everything to me. I love this man without limitations or expectations. He is a man with power during the day and a heart that is as soft as the puffy white clouds up above when he comes home at night. My husband is a thief, a killer, has a filthy mouth with no chance of filtering it, but he's loyal to this family, and our daughter's and my happiness and safety is what makes the love I have for him extend beyond any word created.

So many things have changed in my life after the day I found out my dad didn't lie about being a consultant, he just failed to mention to his little girl he killed people with a gun, or a knife, or, at times, his fist, then disposed of their bodies as if they never existed. Nonetheless, he's my dad, this is my life, and I'm proud to lead it.

All of my changes have been for the good and what is best for my family and me. I'm a lawyer. A female consigliere. To some mafia families, that may be unheard of, a woman being a leader per se in her underground family. Some of them still adhere to the woman's place being to support her husband and keeping her mouth shut. Speak only when you are spoken to, do what you are told. Fucking fools. Who gives a shit about the way others work for their leadership? There are no rules, no margins that state a woman is to stay at home and cook, clean, and become bored out of her mind while her husband works, unless it's her choice; like the choice my mom made to do just that. Maybe in a family who lives by the old standards, but not ours. We're as traditional as they come when it comes to modern-day life. As loving, giving, and caring as everyday people. We give to charities, go to the supermarket ourselves. Hell, I even clean my house. But if we are crossed, then it's war. We will kill you, and I will fight to make sure your killers will never see a day behind bars. In hindsight, it makes me as ruthless as them. A natural-born killer.

There are other things I've come to learn once I returned to the States after living years in Canada to attend college before I eventually received my law degree here in New York, where we now live. Like finding out my high school friend, Manny, is really my cousin, Roan Diamond. That I have a large extended family. Not all of them are blood, but does that matter? What matters is how you feel in your heart. The love you have for them flows long and deep. That's what family is. That's who we are.

My entire family is here beside me, behind me, all around me. It's a day for mourning. A day none of us will ever forget. For today, we bury my uncle, Salvatore Diamond.

You see, he was murdered. And after today, I will no longer be a lawyer. I will become the Underboss of The Diamond Empire, second-in-command to my cousin, Roan.

Well, and now, that soul my uncle wanted to save lacks all compassion and empathy, except for those surrounding me today. I have no idea what color my soul is anymore. Perhaps red, the color of blood; or blue, the color of stability; green, the color of creativity. It doesn't matter which one I see myself being on a daily basis; when you mix those three colors together, you create black. The color of hatred.

Today is the beginning of the end for anyone involved in my uncle's murder.

I'm going to help kill them all.

ROAN

"Roan, you need to slow down and grieve. Please, come home. Alex and I both need you. Let me take care of you, honey." The sound of her pleading voice has me hanging my head in shame. She's as wounded as I am. More so, really. She's home trying to take care of our son, whom we named after her brother, Alexi, who was murdered in a war we all thought ended. And she's worried about me? God, I love her. I'm over here living in hell when I should be home in heaven. With the two of them. The longer I'm away from them, the more it takes away from my sanity. Without them, I'd be living in eternal hell.

Our son is a handful all on his own. He's smack dab in the middle of the terrible twos and has a mouth and an attitude to go along with it. But hell if I don't love that boy unconditionally and miss him terribly. One of his hugs is exactly what I could use right now to ease my pain; to open my heart to his youth, his innocence, and his inability to have a damn clue what the hell is going on around him. To be free. To have him catch my face in between his tiny, uncorrupted hands and squeeze until I make those goofy fish lips that have him laughing uncontrollably. To read to him. To watch cartoons and to take in his face while he learns and lives his life without obstruction. He learns something new every day, and here I am, missing it.

Alina, my stunning wife, has given me the space I've needed up until now. I haven't kissed her lips, touched her body, or climbed inside of my place called heaven in weeks. Not that the urge isn't there every minute of the day. Christ, one look from her sultry eyes, and I'm on my knees, worshipping every part of her tantalizing body. Fucking her dirty, filthy, and making her scream one night, then the next making love to her mind, body, and soul while I whisper those low words of seduction into her ear that send shivers down her spine.

Instead, here I am, shuffling through papers, dealing with my dad's will and racking my brain trying to figure out what crazy son of a bitch put a bullet through my dad's skull, taking him away from his family; stealing his life for reasons unknown to me and every one of us who loved him.

I've been at my parents' home for ten days. That's too long to be away from them and them from me. Her plea shatters my frozen heart into tiny crystals that scatter like a virus, sending remorse throughout my body. Sure, I could have them come here and stay with me. But what good would it do? I wouldn't be spending any time with them anyway.

"I'll be home later tonight, baby. I love you both so much. Kiss him goodnight for me, okay?" I tell her before I hang up and toss my phone on the desk in my dad's office. My hands start to shake right along with my trembling body.

And grieve, she says? Who gives a shit if I've skipped the first two stages of grieving and went right to the third, the one of anger, frustration, and bitterness. I've been grieving since I received the phone call from my father-in-law, Ivan, that my dad had been shot. Right through his head. Dead in an instant by some unwise motherfucker, who now has a price tag on him. Whom I vow to kill myself. To make him suffer in ways no human has suffered before. To make him bleed while I gut him right down to his bones. To have him look at me with fear, knowing he's going to die but suffer before he does. By the time I'm finished with him, and whoever else had their hands in on my beloved dad's brutal murder, they will wish to God they never heard of the name Roan Diamond. I will make them pay. Eternally rock them to the depths of hell.

They say the hardest thing in the world is for a parent to bury their child. Statistics are full of motherfucking shit. Have any of them had to bury a parent? Sit there and watch your mother completely fall apart? Watch her scream, "Why?" over and over? Hold her as she cries and trembles in your arms? Stand helplessly as she loses her goddamn mind? Let her beat her hands on your chest until she falls lax in your arms from pure bodily exhaustion? I fucking doubt it. So screw them and their statistical lies and those who mimic them like they're a fact when I call fucking bullshit. Unless those analysts have felt and experienced it, they don't know a damn thing. They can all take their figures they write down and wipe their asses with them.

Speaking of wiping ass. I need to find this cocksucker who has fucked up my family's world, who has denied my son the right to remember his grandfather, who made my mother a widow and made me lose a man I had the utmost respect for: my father, my idol, the man who has influenced me more than any other. God, I miss him. Ever so wise, always controlled, with a demeanor that demanded respect. He was a fair man unless you crossed him, then you became a dead man. He taught me every damn thing I've become knowledgeable about in this life.

I know more than anyone I'm failing as a husband and father right now. However, as a son to a man who turned me into the man I am, I have a legacy to live up to by filling his shoes and making him proud. Failure doesn't exist in this time of my life I would give anything not to be living. I won't give up until I've made that man proud. Not fucking ever. No matter how badly Alina wants me home right now, she would never expect me to give up this legacy or to find the person responsible for tearing us down.

I'm here for more whys and wherefores I care to count too. First and foremost, I need to keep an eye on my mom, who's so drugged up and out of her mind, I'm not sure she even knows what the hell is going on. One minute she does, the next she's screaming for him. Begging him to come home.

I'm also working from his office, because I feel close to him here, which in my current state of mind is not the smartest thing to do, but it's the only option I've got. If I were to sit back and let the fond memories of Salvatore Diamond surface, the perfect father, friend, and leader, I would crumble. All my strength would stray to putting that shattered heart back together. I'd have nothing left to find his killer. Not to mention losing my shit in front of associates, soldiers, and anyone we do business with is not the right thing to do. Sure, they're all giving me the respect to mourn the loss of the legendary Salvatore Diamond. But it won't be long now before they are knocking on my door to test my strength, to try my weakness, and to offer help. To peel back layers on my ripe flesh to see if I'm filled with fear or if I'm as sour as a rotten apple. I'm neither. They'll be surprised when they find out I'm fearless of them all, filled with revenge and focused on killing someone who branded his own death. They will also find a man who has changed in these past few weeks. I have become bitter and angry, and I don't trust a goddamn one of them. They will all be exposed to the brutal shock of Roan Diamond once they've prodded away at my sanity, tried to make me feel naked and vulnerable. The loyal ones will be pleasantly surprised, while those who are slithering snakes will find out I'm full of nothing but a poisonous venom that's designed to bring whoever betrayed my family down.

This is what my dad would want me to do. I may be going about it in the wrong way at the moment by shutting myself in this room and allowing Cain, Aidan, and my cousin, Dilan, to completely rule our temple of gun trading. They are the ones making sure our shipments are in the right hands and not some narcissistic cult which hates everyone except those who live among them. We've always been particular about who gets our weapons; where they go from the time they leave our hands to theirs, I have no clue. Don't want to know either.

My brothers and cousin are the only ones I trust to do right by my dad and his empire until I have the evidence I need. Then it's all holds barred. All of it will stop, and they will gladly help me kill.

My duties right now are here, in this house, where I can keep a watch on my mom and feel close to my dad at the same time. Where I can utilize my brain and go over every bit of information I can find in all of these files that were locked with a security code on his computer. Everything he had is locked down tight. Two people know the passwords to his computer and safe: me and Uncle John.

Which leads me to this. My theory is one of these motherfuckers who will try to kiss my ass by offering their support or guidance or even their fucked-up theories of suspicion is the man who either pulled the trigger himself or hired someone else. It's that or someone my dad has no clue he crossed, a bitter battle someone couldn't let go of. Was he killed by association? Meaning that bullet was meant for Ivan? These theories are nagging at me like a plague targeting my soul. Until I have proof in the palm of my hands, not one of them can be trusted. The only ones I trust are Cain, Aidan, and Dilan, Uncle John, Ivan, and my cousin, Calla, in this leadership circle. The rest of them are all on my radar. All within sucking in the last breath they will take in this polluted world we live in. The air will become clean, revenge will be had, and until that day comes, I will become gritty and uncompromising; and if I suspect them, then I will rip every limb off their body, feed it to the sharks, and watch the hungry beasts devour their body as if they never existed. The day will come when they will be persecuted and wish they chose to walk a straight life of purification instead of one of tainted corruption and dishonor. They will rot from their own stench, while revenge pumps through my veins as if I'm ready to explode from a lethal combination of drugs that turns a person into a ballistic maniac. My high won't come down until my hallucinations are a reality. And the need to kill is the only thing to cure me of the addiction.

I would be entirely lost in this cesspool of indestructible hate if it weren't for my uncle and Ivan guiding me through this shit, breaking down enemies from years ago to today, crossing people off the list, adding new ones to it daily. My uncle may be retired, but he sure as hell knows what the fuck is going on, and Ivan is torrential with his knowledge of whom he trusts and whom he doesn't. I can only hope to be as well-informed as the two of them one day. And still, with the three of us putting our heads together, we are left with nothing except whoever did this is a pro. Someone with a clean shot, a steady finger, and protection even I can't infiltrate.

"You should go home, get cleaned up. Spend time with your family. Besides, isn't that the same shirt you had on yesterday?" Calla gnashes out at me as she enters the office and slams the door shut behind her. Christ, she's a blessing for my tired and weary eyes, but she looks as beat down as I do. I'm not about to tell her that though, because she's diving into the same deep shit I am, only it's going to be deeper for her. These men who I was just thinking about will tear her apart before they are convinced she should stand by my side, where she rightfully belongs.

Her eyes scan the entirety of the room. I have photos everywhere. Each one is identifying a possible suspect. Any man my dad may have crossed since the first day he joined the syndicate lifestyle. I even have death certificates, marriage licenses, and birth certificates of every motherfucker I can think of. And not a goddamn one of them leads me to the person I've stretched my brain to the capacity of exploding looking for.

"I could ask you the same thing. And for your information, no, this is not the same shirt. I may have all these voices talking to me at the same damn time, driving me bat shit crazy, but I do shower and change my clothes. I eat too," I simply state and gesture with a flip of my hand toward the empty plate next to me my aunt brought in a few hours ago. Then I lean back in the chair with a smug look on my face. Calla has been busting her ass as much as I have. Unlike me, she has the luxury of doing it from home, where she can be with her daughter. Where she should be. Instead of working at our law firm, she has shoved her entire career to the side to stand beside me as my second-in-command. To serve her family. This is not the way my dad would have wanted this. Of course, this legacy carries on with Calla and me. But she's no use to any of us if she winds up dead. If they smell she's weak, I won't be able to protect her like I used to. They will destroy her before she even begins. Break her. Besides, I'll be buried right next to her if anyone touches a hair on her head. Cain will kill me himself. I know he hates the idea of her becoming our underboss. He knows it's her duty. Doesn't mean he has to like it. I'm there with him. In fact, I hate it. Hate is so much that once Aidan returns from California in a few days, he'll be sticking to her like she's the only thing that matters. Cain volunteered to do it at first. His eyes were flaming with rage when I shot him down. Not a chance in hell was I allowing that to happen. We're all close to one another, but a husband protecting his wife only leads to one thing: death by destruction. He'd end up getting both of them killed. He can protect her at home, at night, when their house is locked down tighter than a maximum-security prison. Which reminds me, how the hell did she get here and where is Justice? I know Alina is locked in tight at our home. Guards are surrounding our house; at the gate, at every door. Fucking hell, our freedom to roam has been obliterated by this cocksucker.

"Well, you look like shit," she spews the truth. I feel like shit too; I haven't slept in God knows how long. Most of it's because I hover over my mother whenever I hear her in the bedroom she shared for years with my dad. I swear to God every tear she sheds drives the knife farther into my heart. It's impossible to help her. To know what to say and what to keep from her. Thank fuck for Aunt Cecily, who goes back and forth between her place to here every day to help. She's another blessing. She's also Calla's mother. Calla gets her strength and determination from both my aunt and uncle. A callous woman in the courtroom, she's nicknamed The Lady of Liberty. She's soulless when it comes to her job, firing her knowledge at you like a malfunctioned machine gun, one rapid bullet after another. Drilling holes without blinking an eye. But when it comes to her family, she's a tenderhearted, faithful, loyal woman. I have no doubt whoever did this, she will be honored to help destroy them.

I ignore her comment and dive right into chewing her ass out. She knows it's not safe right now for her to be out and about, making herself an open target to our enemy.

"How the hell did you get here?" I stand and grip the desk, white knuckling it and all.

"Settle down, for goodness sake. Cain brought me here. He took Justice upstairs to see your mom. I'm hoping seeing her will make her feel better. He'll be down here in a few minutes. I'm not stupid, Roan. I know it's dangerous for me to be out, but I had to come." I rear my head back at her abrasive remark.

"I know you're not stupid. Far from it, but I thought I asked you to stay home to deal with turning all your clients over to someone else in the firm, and I would come to you when I had information to share. It's dangerous for you to be visible right now, Calla."

"You know what, Roan?" She leans in and mocks my stare quite convincingly. If I didn't know her, I might be intimidated by her badass vigilante attitude that reminds me of the famous Boudica, who they say slaughtered an entire Roman empire after her husband's murder. It's not me she has to convince. It's the other families that will push her, try to

13

break her, and they will do everything they can to try and eat her alive. She'll be threatened, interrogated by every one of them until she either breaks or convinces them she is one bitch they don't want to mess with.

Maybe she's testing her capabilities out on me, showing me she can handle the gruesome side of this business instead of being the one who represents murderers, thieves, and computer hackers. You name the crime, and we've all pretty much committed it. I'm just lucky enough to have ever been caught. Don't plan to be either. I have no idea what's roaming around in her head. I'm about to flip on her though. Give her the largest dose of reality she will get. Family or not, she needs to prepare herself for the unexpected at any given time.

"I'm hurting too. We all are. We will never recover from this loss. But when I receive a phone call from your wife, who happens to be worried about you by the way, I will risk it to check on you. Pull your head out of your ass. When we're done here, you need to go the hell home, Roan." A cold, straightforward smirk stretches across her mouth she spews from, although those eyes of hers are calling the shots right now as they shoot missiles right into mine by the way she stares me down fearlessly. Good girl. *Don't back down. Not even from me, Calla*, I think to myself.

The mere mention of my wife claws across my heart to back down from giving her a test of my own. I refuse. This war is going to be ugly. Calla wants in; she better let my words hit the first layer of her skin and penetrate to the deepest level of her bones. It better mix in with her marrow and make her fearless. Make her stand her ground. Make her use her knowledge in a courtroom to tear these motherfuckers apart. Because not all families are like ours. They will cut your throat and bleed you dry. It doesn't matter to them whether that blood they watch pouring out of you is the same blood running through their veins. Their greed for power and money are more important to them than anything. Both Calla and I know this with the hell we went through all those years ago with my brother, Royal. He nearly killed us both over his hunger to control this family. To take what he thought was rightfully his.

I'll give her credit for coming here and tossing my weakness in my face. She knows good and well how important my family is to me. I breathe for my wife and son, and now as the boss of this empire, I will lay my life down for every member of this family. Blood or not.

I'll be damned if the conversation that needs to happen between Calla and me is over. And fucking Cain. His ass needs to be around to get the big picture too. I don't give one fuck who she is or if she tries to manipulate or undermine her husband into bringing her here or taking her to the fucking supermarket. She will stay put until I feel it's safe for her to exist beyond the realms of her home.

Her new home at that. They were the last ones to move out of the apartment building we'd all lived in. Now, all of us live in the same gated community. We wanted our children to grow up with a yard to play in, fur babies to chase around, and to become playmates, soul mates, and brothers and sisters for life like all of their parents are. And now, fuck all if my son can't even play on his new backyard play set or chase our little Dachshund, Peanut, around outside. Or swim. Or do anything a normal child should be able to do in the safety of his own atmosphere.

Alina and I moved first, followed by Dilan and Anna. Then, after she twisted his arm several times, Deidre finally talked Aidan into moving again. Hell, she's pregnant with their third child already. These women and children need to remain safe. Out of sight. Especially Calla.

I take a deep breath, trying to calm the torment of all turmoil that is banning me from my family being able to live like normal people before I give my cousin more than she can handle. "Calla. I appreciate you checking up on me and being concerned about Alina. But I haven't been able to leave my mom. She's broken. I know I will never be able to fix her, to put her back together again. She took care of me when I couldn't take care of myself. She needs me here. I need to be close to her. If I could have them here with me, I would. Hell, I'd have all of us here, but

I can't. I need to focus on what needs to be done here. I'm not sure what else I can say or do to make all of you grip a hold of the severity of this. None of us are safe. Especially you and me. These men from the other syndicates are going to tear you apart. You'll be the one on trial here. They'll interrogate you. Demean you. Test you." I'm raising my voice, because I sense she's ready to cut me off, to speak her mind before I'm finished. "Some of these men are old school. They don't think the way we do about women. Women do not equal up to them. They're old, decrepit bastards who think women have no rights, and they will eat you alive if they smell any sign of weakness on you. Do you get what the hell I'm saying here?"

Instead of her staring back at me with absorbing fright, she spins the bottle in my direction and moves her face in closer. Her intimidating stare squares off with an expression mirroring mine.

"You are so wrong, Roan. It's our courtroom. These men are on trial here with me being the judge and you being the jury. They have no say over what happens with the Diamond Empire. That decision is up to you and me. I'm new blood to them, and I get it. I'm also very aware I'm a woman. A woman with an intuition that one of these sons of bitches ordered that hit. I can pick out a liar before he or she even speaks. You're going to want me by your side more than you're going to need me there. I've represented the guilty, remember? My life is in jeopardy every day, and if you think I'm backing off now, then you don't know me at all." Oh. I know her, all right. This woman, who thinks she's seen it all, may be the one who exemplifies crimes that are so inhuman they would make a normal person want to slice their throat. But now, those crimes will happen right in front of her. She'll witness shit she's never seen before. Not even the hell my brother tried to put the two of us through comes close to what her eyes will testify to. She has one chance to prove she can show how courageous she thinks she'll be. Only one.

"Fear isn't in our blood, Roan. I'm as much a part of this nuclear-powered family as everyone else. I'll kill anyone who attempts to take another person I love away from me. Now, we have a few hours left before you go home to the dinner your wife is making. The dinner I promised her you would be at. Let's get to fucking work." She puffs out a long breath, leans in, and with one clean swipe of her hand, she shoves the papers in front of me to the side. Half of them scatter to the floor. "You won't be needing those," she speaks in a bossy tone, "if my theory is correct. I believe I've found the man we're looking for."

CALLA

Roan's words of danger have the conversation Deidre and I had the night we buried my uncle running through my head. "These people are ruthless, Calla. Are you sure you can handle it?" I told her as well as Alina and Anna the same thing I'm telling Roan. I'm extremely aware of how dangerous this situation is. I may not have had the displeasure of personally dealing with these wretched leaders who don't play fair in our world; on the contrary, I will not tolerate any of them treating me any different because I have tits and a vagina. If it weren't for women, they would be fucking each other over more than they do now. Welcome to the first episode of badassery and women power, you self-righteous dicks.

I'm a firm believer in women's rights. I don't care what men's opinions are of us or what a woman is trying to accomplish. We are all equal. The only difference we have is, women use their brain the way we should, while most men use what hangs between their legs to do their bidding for them. And I can guarantee, these overbearing suckers have dicks that should be playing a role in Ripley's Believe it or Not. Small dicks, small brains, and all that jazz.

I've been fighting round after round with Cain for weeks over this. The need to protect me I get. We have a daughter, is his argument. "Why do you feel the need to take on this role? You don't have to, you know? One of us can." It's not that Cain wants this position. No. That's not it at all. The man is scared of losing his wife. Of the things I will see, the things I may have to do. How I'll react to being threatened. Will the same thing or worse happen to me like it did before? It's not one bit funny, but the only way to shut that man up is to flash my tits and vagina in his face. Then fuck him until his cock—which isn't small by any means—takes over his worried brain. Like I said, *men*. I love my man though. These pissy, arrogant cock-suckers who will be calling a meeting at any time are the worthless pieces of shit. Except the Solokovs, who think in this century and treat everyone equally like we do, not like these fools who I've studied until my eyes were bleeding and could no longer make out their faces through my blurred vision. Most of them I haven't met yet, and they already make me sick and make me want to hurl all over their expensive Armani suits. They could all learn a thing or two from a woman.

"Get to the point, Calla. You said we don't have time to fuck around. Let me hear your theory."

"You need to loosen up, Roan. You sound like Hitler, for god's sake." I salute him.

The tiny crack of a smile he had moments ago falls; in its place is the face of a man who's suffered loss and hardship. This look on him is what I hate. I've been busting my ass to help him out here. Searching through tiny holes for any goddamn thing I could find.

What Cain and Roan don't understand is the craving I have to protect them too. It's my right. I may not have lived my entire life growing up in this environment of murder, drugs, stealing, and the latest, underground illegal fighting, but I'm no fool. I can play with fire, but I'm not allowing myself to get burned.

"I'm not afraid of those men, you know. I'm not afraid of you either. In fact, I just may be your biggest weapon. Remember that, Roan," I seethe. Between him and Cain trying to scare the crap out of me, I'm ready to prove myself to them more than anyone else.

The sharp tongue, piss, and vinegar are all in my blood. Just like Roan, I will kill for my blood. I also know Roan. That man protects with his life, as do the rest of these men. He's going to have someone on me at all times. Maybe even several men. What he fails to realize is, my dad will never allow anything to happen to me. He's already volunteered to go where I go. People are scared to death of the unstoppable John Greer, and they should be. He's killed and made more people disappear than I want to know about, but he's my father, my protector, and even though I trust our friends and family, I trust him more. His eyes are everywhere, trained on point. I don't want anything to happen to my dad. I do know he will refuse to let anyone take care of what's his, especially after the hell I went through with Roan's older brother, Royal; a man I didn't know before he kidnapped me. Besides, both of them know my dad has trained me to shoot. *I hope I remember how.* I'm not invincible, none of us are. But I sure as hell will not lie down and let anyone trample all over me. Especially men who don't respect me.

I'm sick and tired of this shit. Here we think everything is fine. That people will stick with the rules. You stay in your territory, and I'll stay in mine. Hell no, someone crossed over. Someone shot my uncle in cold blood. All of our men knew what kind of rifle was used before the forensics reports came back. After all, that is what they do: steal, smuggle, and sell them. Someone hired a pro to snipe off the man who always treated me like his daughter, who accepted my husband and me, who helped protect me when I never knew I needed to be protected all those years ago when I was on my own in college. Whoever hired this person knew exactly what they were doing. They used a Ruger Precision

Rifle, American made, to either throw us off and make us think it came from within our family or another American syndicate. Those guns are our top moneymakers. I don't buy it for one second. My suspicions tell me otherwise. I believe it's the new crime family that's brought their underground fighting to the States. For whatever reason, they considered my uncle a threat. With my brains and the influence Roan has, we will sit down and figure this shit out. Then we'll plan, kill, and send their souls to the devil.

I sigh as Roan tries to scare me. If it weren't for the fact I want him to go home, to try and be as normal as he can be until we derive a plan and set it in motion, I would challenge him more. I love him. He's the only true family I have, and I want him to grieve the loss, let my dear, sweet friend take her husband and guide him through this.

I refuse to fight with my cousin or my husband any more about this. We need to stand united and prove to these men that no matter what they think of me, our family is stronger than we've ever been, and there isn't a damn thing they can do to try and break us.

"You can't have theories, Calla, and you know it. You of all people should know we need facts before we accuse anyone. Solid fucking proof. You want to spend time with me scouring through every crooked cop, politician, and anyone else my dad has come in contact with, then by all means, have at it. I've seen their faces more times than I care to." Roan takes his hand and flings it around this unorganized office. I want to smirk and scream 'girl power.'

"Roan. I'm a lawyer. We strive on theories, we pursue them, investigate, and," I point my finger in his direction, "if we're good, which I am by the way, our theories turn into evidence that wins our case." He may be smart in the areas he has been trained in; well, so am I. He knows it. I'll strike his comment up to the fact he's overly exhausted, misses his family, and needs to go home. I'm going to lay it out for him in black and white. Or in this case, color. I turn around and walk to my briefcase I flung on the leather sofa when I walked in, unlock the combination, then run my hands over the smooth leather and flip open the lid.

Right on top is the photo of the man I believe to be responsible, or at least think had something to do with it. I retrieve it along with the thick file, close it back up, and make my way back. As I go to sit down, I toss the file first on the desk in front of him, followed by the photo. Roan's expression changes from confusion to anger when he stares down at the photo of Donald Sweeney, Jr., or 'Donal' for short. The thirty-one-year-old son of the late Donald Sweeney, who once claimed he wanted to rule the underground world. He died of a heart attack five years ago, shortly after he moved to the States to begin his underground fighting. He was a ruthless man. Said to be one of the few men to have little or no remorse if one of his fighters were to be killed in the ring. If they tap out or lose, they are considered weak. He then decides their fate. His men are basically trained to kill in that ring. No knock out in this type of fighting. They kill with their bare hands by strangling or beating them half to death; by a snap of the neck or a punch to the susceptible spot on the temple that can kill you; by a heart punch or a direct blow to the kidneys. It's all there, every word. Every unfortunate death. And we know Donal has brought this fighting from Chicago to New York. He's involved. I know he is.

"Jesus Christ." Roan starts flipping through the pages, glancing and reading, while I sit there stoically and study his face. I love analyzing people. Roan is an enigma though, always has been. He's damn good at what he does but not afraid at all to speak his mind or to show his anger and frustration; he simply doesn't care what others think of him. He is what he is: loyal and honorable. He will make a remarkable leader. Those are only a few of the reasons why he's respected in a world full of evil and corruption, deceit, and debauchery. Love versus hate.

"I've studied these photos. I've researched this rat bastard who wants to try and finish off what his father could not. Now it's up to you to explore my theory, to lead us into where we go from here." He briefly scans the next few pages. The closer he gets to the one I'm petrified could send him over the edge, the more my heart shatters due to the memories that will surface for my cousin while he's sitting directly across from me.

He remains quiet as he precisely studies every line, every note I've written down.

"This is what I mean about the brains behind the brawn, Roan. I'm going on perception here. A hunch. I've been trained to never roll over on a hunch, Roan. NEVER," I emphasize with a brutal punch as if I'm standing in the courtroom hammering away as I'm giving my closing statement to a jury.

"This is your suspect? For fucks sake. Why would he off my dad? We've stayed clear of this shit. His invites have been turned down by us as well as Ivan. Where's the proof, Calla? The goddamn proof?" He runs his hands through his hair. I cross my legs and wait—nervously, I might add—until he comes to the page I need to him see. I cringe inside. I hate this more the closer he gets to the last few photos I discovered that drew my suspicion to this man in the first place. It was the same feeling all over again when I first saw them. My hackles went up, sending me into a frenzy of worry and concern. I've kept this to myself until I investigated every avenue, leaving nothing unturned. I'm as sure of this as I am that I'm breathing.

"Maybe I should have told you sooner, or Cain, but I had to be sure. I wasn't about to get anyone's hopes up or down, or possibly start a war with another family if I wasn't positive." I keep talking to ease the tension creeping up my neck. Even though all my lawyerly instincts tell me this is the stupidity of a crazy man, there isn't a single person in my family who will not put this man under suspicion for what I've found out about him. Plus, even though I loved my uncle, he was Roan's dad, his mentor, his idol, and I want Roan to grieve. Once I found out he was staying here and not at home where he should be, I moved as fast as I could to gather all this information and put it in order to get it to him.

He's going to need Alina more now than he's ever needed her.

"Mother. Fucker. No way. No." He picks up the photos and flings them across the room. This time, I remain silent. Roan has to come to terms with this. He startles me when he glares at me with narrow, cold, and ridged eyes that are slightly brimming with tears. God, I knew this would destroy him. Seeing him like this is choking me up. As his cousin, I want to hold him, comfort him, and tell him we will get through this. As his second-in-command as well as a person who now has to hold every hurting emotion inside of me, I can't. I need to prove to him as well as the men he's warned me about that I can handle this. That I too want this sick fucker buried underground where he belongs.

It's hard to tell what he's thinking when he's staring right through me as if he's remembering, seeing a ghost. His eyes are haunted. I've become invisible to him. It breaks my heart watching him morph back in time. I'm allowing him a few more moments to get a grip on reality, to prove to me he can cope with it. That he will not fly off the handle and kill this man before we investigate this further. It needs to be done with as few people as possible. It also needs to be done with someone Donal doesn't know, which more than likely won't be any of us.

"Roan," I call out with concern. He blinks a few times but doesn't answer me. I inhale deeply before I stand and move around to the side of the desk, where he's gripping hold of it like he's trying to break a solid piece of wood. His knuckles are turning white; his face follows suit. He's turned to ice, a protective shield covering up scars; wounds I can't begin to imagine have got to be opening back up in his head.

"Damn it, Roan." I place my hand over the top of one of his, startled at how cold it feels.

The door stuns me when it opens, and Cain walks in. His features immediately turn from confusion to worry. My husband is an observant man. He knows something isn't right.

He shuts the door behind him and takes a step, which happens to be one that lands his foot directly on top of one of those photos. The crunching noise has three sets of eyes darting down. I close mine briefly, thanking someone above that Roan is finally alert, and when I open them, Cain now has both pictures in his hands, reading the pages stapled to the back of them, the description of who this man is as well as my notes, theories, and the reason why I believe this is who we need to find. His eyes are scurrying back and forth between the two of them. His nostrils flare. His face turns red. I know he wants to curl his fist and ball the evidence in his hands to make them disappear. I watch the anger radiate off of his skin. Pure raw fury stifles this room, hatred so intense that not even the sharpest knife would dull the surface that surrounds me when Roan and Cain's eyes meet. Their motionless gazes are accompanied by a look I've never seen before. It's deeper than rage, stronger than anger. It's the core of it all: fear.

"Babe, please tell me you haven't breathed a goddamn word to anyone about this?" Cain breaks the silence first. His voice is shaky, and those beautiful eyes of his turn to me with a tenacity of fright.

"I haven't spoken to anyone, Cain. Roan deserved to see this first." He nods, and I catch the glimpse of the love that runs deep for me before he trains his troubled eyes back to Roan.

"I'm not going to ask you if you're all right, brother. Clearly, you're not. What I am going to tell you is, you need to go home. Spend some time with Alina and Alex. Don't breathe a word of this to her or anyone. Before you do that, you need to pull your fucking shit together and make a call to Ivan. He needs to know about this. Ask him to set up the meeting. It's time, Roan." His voice is serious. His glare is on fire. *Time for what*? For us to move forward?

Roan still doesn't speak. I believe his silence is a front for the pain, hurt, and anger of a history he thought was dead and buried. His tough exterior is crumbling for the time being. Mine did too but not like his. Never like his.

"Life sure as hell knows how to play the cruel, vicious game of 'Fuck you, Roan', doesn't it?" he whispers.

"No, Roan. You can't think that. None of this is your fault." I lift his hand, entwining our fingers together. Immediately, he jerks away from me, dropping my hand and making me feel like I've burned him.

"It's my fault my dad is dead. It's all my fucking fault." I refuse to allow him to think this. This is one person's fault, for reasons we both know the answers to.

"That's bullshit, and you know it, man. It is not your fault. It's his fault. It all leads back to this crazy motherfucker!" Cain shouts. He jabs his finger toward the man standing next to Donal Sweeney in the picture. The two of them are laughing with one another, chumming it up together.

"Right. It all leads back to him. A phantom of a man who's been dead for years, Cain. A man who haunts us from his grave. Who was obviously a lot smarter than any of us. He plotted and he won, didn't he? He took away one of the only people on this earth who he knew would make me live in regret and agony for the rest of my life. And now what? We play his game again? We fight a war? A war we may never win? Where more people will die? This will never end, will it? He could strike again from his home in hell. He could kill my mom, my wife, my son. You." Roan points a shaky finger at me.

"Then we put a stop to it. We set our revenge. If he were working with any other family, they would have struck us again by now. Your dad was a respected man. He had no issues with anyone. If he did, he would have known. This Irish clan is new to our territory. It's obvious they don't play by the rules. This is a game they can't win, Roan. Every family will stand with us. They're outnumbered here." Anger rolls off of Roan like a mad man setting up home inside his body, scattering his kind across the plains of his features at the command of Cain's words. Sweat forms at his temples. Tears fill his eyes. My heart shatters from watching his expression as he fights against disappearing inside of himself, to rid our family of the parasite who has plagued us from his grave.

"The both of you do me the same favor before this starts. Don't tell anyone about this. Not a soul. If this gets back to my mom or Alina, it will destroy them both. They cannot find out that my brother is the one responsible for my dad's death."

ROAN

My brain is aching. My eyes are on fire. I close my eyes and try to fight off the feeling that someone has purposely strapped me down to blind me. Tiny drops feel like they are dripping into my eyes. The poison is stinging and burns my throat when I try to swallow. It's a lethal combination that's draining my mind from anything else except for what they want me to remember. *My brother.*

My sick, fucking, twisted brother and this bastard Donal Sweeney derived a plan to take out my dad long after my brother's death, and I want to know why that fucker waited so long to attack my family, or why he did it all. What goddamn kind of game is this? Years! My brother has been dead for years! And what in the hell is going to happen next? Are there more of us they plan on taking out? What does the slimy weasel think he has accomplished by starting a fighting battle he has to know he'll lose? I've heard of his temper, his drill, and the way he conducts his business. He's a shady cocksucker, one not to be trusted.

He muscled into the state of New York by buying his way in with all the greedy motherfuckers who love to watch people beat the hell out of each other for money. My dad, nor Ivan, wanted anything to do with him. He's twisted. Word on the street is, he loves to take his frustrations out on women by smacking them around. Any man who touches a woman in any other way except to cherish her is a straight-up pussy. I'd give anything to get that fucker into one of his rings myself. Kill him with my hands and fuck him up until he's begging me to kill him off.

I'm determined more than ever to figure out a way to find this cocksucker; to put his organization on public display. I don't care if he pads the wallets of these citizens. I want the Irish crime unit the fuck out of my city.

There's no doubt he knows everything there is to know about us. Bringing in any one of my guys would get them killed before they crossed through the door. He has to be suspicious of us, watching us. "Mother. Fucker," I whisper, my fingers tapping on the window in perfect rhythm to the tap, tap of my brain.

He killed the wrong man in this crime world of ours. There isn't a single leader out there who would back this scum up. He has to know we won't stop until we take him out. It's obvious he knew where dad was that night to have him killed in cold blood outside of a restaurant in downtown Manhattan. The only thing I can thank the piece of shit for is, Dad and Ivan were having a friendly dinner alone; the two of them weren't out with my mom and mother-in-law. That right there would have destroyed my mom more than losing her soul mate has. To see his life snuffed out right in front of her. Fuck, he could have taken her out too.

Calla came through with the information we needed. For the sake of the two women I love most in this world, I wish to God what she found out was a lie. That a man could hate so much that even from his grave he has the power to destroy us. The woman is a hell of a lot tougher than I gave her credit for. Shit, she stood strong while I wanted to crumble and scream and get the answers I've wanted my entire life. Why and how could a man hate his family the way my brother hated all of us? How could he destroy the woman who gave him life, to have her live out the rest of her days without her husband? Never mind how the man cared about me. He's hated me since the day I was born. My own goddamn sibling. Fucking hell.

And now, here I am on my way home to lie to my wife after the three of us cleaned up my mess. Calla and Cain took every bit of the information I had strewn around the office home with them, while I have the file she assembled tucked and locked away in my briefcase. God forbid my mom goes into that room and finds anything that would hurt her more. I lied to my mom before I walked out her door, telling her I'm still as far away from finding out who's responsible as I was yesterday. It's easy to lie to a woman who's drugged up on a sedative to calm her and help her sleep; but to lie to a woman who knows you better than anyone else and watches your every move, waiting for you to hit rock bottom, is another thing. My wife is very in tune with my every move right now, waiting for me to grieve, to cry. To let it all out.

"Goddamn it." I punch the back of the seat, startling my driver, Lenny. He's one of the few people I trust outside of the inner circle of leaders in the family. The man is pushing seventy years; he's been my dad's driver for twenty-five years, and now he's mine. I would have asked him to retire or keep him around for social gatherings, charities, and functions that Alina and I will attend. I've grown accustomed to driving myself around, but with not knowing if my life is safe or not, I decided it was best to have him drive me.

"Just a few more steps, Dad, and you would have made it to the safety of this car."

Lenny's eyes catch mine in the review mirror as we sit at the stoplight. My words are causing him pain and guilt. He was off that night on a family outing.

"Shit, Lenny. I'm sorry. I didn't mean…"

"I know what you meant, Roan. Doesn't make the guilt go away now, does it?"

"No, it doesn't. Nothing will." That's the goddamn truth. I will live the rest of my life with one form of guilt or another always ready to crawl out of its hole and smother me.

Lenny has heard and seen more in the years our family has employed him than anyone else. He knows I've learned something, and yet for the longest time neither one of us speaks, not until he shocks me with his words.

"A piece of advice, Roan, if I may?" he politely asks. He averts his eyes back to the road as we speed off toward my home.

"You've been dishing out wise words to me since before I knew what the hell you were talking about, Lenny. Don't stop now." Even though the car has darkened from pulling onto the highway, the streetlights left far behind, I still feel a slight tug at the corners of his lips, and knowing this old man as I do, I'm in for some well-needed advice. I lean my head back on the cool leather seat and close my eyes as I listen to the wise words from a wise man.

"Your dad was proud of you, boy. And I'm not talking about a damn thing that has to do with running this business. I'm talking about you. The man you are. You're loyal, faithful, and trustworthy. I see so much of him in you. His determination and his need to fix things; to make sure those you love live in peace." He pauses. I inhale deeply, soaking in his words, letting them seep into my bones as visions of my father and me, as so many memories wash over me. A son remembering his dad, his voice, his praises, and the way his face would light up whenever he saw Alex. Him giving me a hug for the simple fact I was his son and he loved me. Memorable. Cherished.

"Your dad and I have had many talks over the years, Roan. During the same conversation we had many times while he sat in the very same spot as you, he asked me to look out for you if anything were to happen to him. To be the man you needed when everyone else around you is dedicated to doing what needs to be done, all the while hating it but doing it anyway. I made that promise to him at lease a hundred times. It was an easy one, because I too love the man you are. The point I am making is, whatever you have found out, make sure the plan you have to put an end to it is done when you are ready. Don't blame yourself, Roan. Be the man your dad knew you to be. A man reliable enough to make sure this war ends in your favor. That justice is done the way you want it done." Relief sweeps over me as his words slam into my gut. I squeeze my eyes shut tighter to blink back the tears I have yet to shed. *Fuck, what kind of man doesn't cry over the death of his father? One who hasn't had time to grieve, that's who.* I need my wife.

"You're a wise man, Lenny." I tell him the god's honest truth. I run my hand across the seat while I rest my arm on the sill of the door, right here in this spot where my father planned and talked with one of the few people he knew he could trust. I take a deep breath before I share the information I have learned with a man whose eyes have witnessed, whose ears have heard, and whose mouth gives me a missing piece of this jagged puzzle when I'm done telling him everything. I spill my guts out to Lenny, and he in return gives me hope. "Lenny," I say with purpose. "Are you offering me your son for our way into the Irish mob? I don't think this is what Dad had in mind when he asked you to look out for me," I articulate.

"No, it wasn't. That's not the question in hand here though, is it? Look," he says. I hear his brain working as he tries to convince me that a young man would be willing to give up his life of normalcy in order to dive into a corrupted world he knows nothing about. It's going to take a hell of a lot more than what he's saying now.

"I'm not throwing my son out there to be killed. I trust you, Roan. I trust your ability to keep him safe. What I am doing is giving you the inside you need. Just talk to him. Hear him out. I think you'll be surprised that there are more people willing to help you than you realize," he tells me convincingly.

"It's tempting, Lenny. But I won't put anyone in danger unless they know how to defend themselves. I need proof he can. Proof he has the guts to handle the kind of shit that goes on inside one of those fights. Proof he can defend himself when all hell breaks loose. Because we both know if this Donal is responsible for the death of my dad, it will. Show me proof, and then I'll give you my answer."

It's almost midnight by the time we arrive at my home. The driveway is lit up, and security is standing guard. Shards of guilt hit me all over again thinking how dangerous it is for my son to play outside. Pisses me the hell off, the fact he may never lead a normal life. I wonder if he'll want to take over the realms someday or be a doctor like his mother, or an accountant, or if he'll wash his hands of me, tell me he wants nothing to do with me after he's old enough to understand his old man is a killer, a thief, and disobeys the law.

"Thank you, Lenny. You drive safe now. We'll talk soon." I lean forward, squeezing his shoulder before I exit the car.

"Take the time you need, Roan. Leave the rest to me." He pats my hand then puts the car back into drive. I take that as my sign to get out of the car. I grab my briefcase, open the door, and watch him pull away. I'm restless, exhausted, and eager to see my family.

I climb the few stairs leading into my house. All I want to do is inhale my son's innocent scent, kiss the hell out of my wife, and bury myself inside of her. My family. My home. It's everything.

It's quiet when I enter. I reset the alarm and smile when I see my boy's trucks up and down the hallway, and his little tennis shoes stuffed in the corner. I kick my shoes off and place them along with my briefcase next to his, ascend the stairs, and walk right to his room, where he's tucked into his small Batmobile bed. This boy has one hell of a room. The entire walls are painted to look like Gotham City.

"If only Batman could save our family and this city, buddy." I bend down and kiss his dark, curly-haired head. I have no idea how long I stand and watch him in his peaceful sleep. When I turn around, I'm met by the most beautiful, intoxicating woman I have ever had the privilege of setting my eyes on. The moonlight on her long, blonde hair has my palms itching to tug it back and devour her neck, to trail down to where those nipples are peeking out of the thin shirt, to travel lower to my kingdom, my heaven. Christ, she's taken this exhausted man and turned him into a man whose cock has hardened in an instant. I am wide-awake.

"Hey, lover," she whispers seductively.

"Hey, Mrs. Diamond. I'm sorry I didn't make dinner." She shrugs, the shirt falling off her shoulder when it lifts. Fuck me. I look her up and down respectively yet hungry as an animal that comes out at night to eat its prey. I silently close the door behind me, and just like that animal, I snatch her into my arms and haul her over my shoulder. That ass I've had many times is there, and I swear to God, it's tempting as fuck to take it right now. Her ass isn't the part of her I crave though; I crave her pussy. The way it smells, tastes, and grips me like her life depends on it. Mine depends on it. On her. On this life we're building together.

"I missed you," she tells me when I enter our room, kick the door shut, and toss her sweet little ass on the bed. I'm on her before I answer, thankful it's dark so she can't see my tormented face. My mouth is all over her slim, delicate neck. My hands are in her hair. My jean-covered cock is pressing into her heat.

"Oh God, Roan." My name coming from her mouth enthralls me. The way she says my name is the sweetest thing I've heard in weeks. I trail up her jaw and hover my lips over hers, wanting to utter those words I've been craving to say as I stare at her beautiful orbs watching me, waiting for her to say it back.

"I fucking love you so damn much," I express.

"I love you too." I'm silent for a moment while I listen to her unsteady breathing, while I feel the beat of her heart beneath me. After regaining my senses, relief absorbs my mind that I'm home. I consume her mouth. I'm not messing around here; I fuck her mouth with my tongue. It's everywhere, as is hers. Darting, licking, and worshipping each other like we always do. She's the only one who can make me forget. The only one I need.

When her hand slips between us and grips my cock, I moan into her mouth, gripping her bare ass as I do. I fucking love it when I come home to her naked underneath one of my old, ratted high school t-shirts she hoarded when we moved in together. Sexiest damn thing I've seen her wear. Except me.

"You hungry?" she teases as she traces my bottom lip with that crafty little tongue of hers.

"I'm hungry to taste you and then fuck." My body grows with anticipation when she unzips my pants and grabs a hold of me. Squeezing. I nip her lip while she strokes my cock. Because it's been days since I've been inside of her, I pull away before I blow my load in her hand, sit up, and tug my shirt over my head. By the time I'm standing and have disposed of my jeans and boxers, my wife has her shirt off, her hands palm her tits, and fuck me like crazy, the moonlight shadowing her has me mesmerized. If I didn't want to taste her so bad, I would stand here and jerk my cock all over her while she played with those sweet tits of hers.

"Don't you dare take those hands of those tits. I want those pink nipples hard, Alina. I want you squirming underneath me, coming on my face, and saying my name."

I grab her by the ankles, spreading her legs and skimming my hands all the way up until they meet her hot, wet pussy. The warmth radiating off of her sends me into a tailspin. She's as hungry for me as I am for her. Damn vixen. She gasps like it's the first time I'm tossing around my domineering ways with her. I may take control most of the time in our bed, but when a man loves his wife as much as I do mine, he'd be a fool to think he's really the one in control. I'll be the first person to admit Alina rules me; she just chooses to put me first, to let me think I hold all the power. God, I love her.

"I need this," I simply say. She knows though that tonight won't be gentle and sweet. Not that she minds at all. Alina and I have no boundaries in this bed whatsoever. We explore and experience, at times, we fuck each other raw, while at others, we make love. It's a variable sex life, fulfilling, and Christ almighty, it is the best feeling in the world to crave someone so much that your entire performance is based on pleasing them.

"Not as bad as I want you. Oh shit, Roan." Her hips jerk up.

"Yeah, you want it. You been playing with this pussy too while I've been gone. I know I've jerked my cock every night dreaming of this."

"You know I did. But it doesn't feel as good as you."

"Don't I fucking know it."

My head dips down to replace my hand, inhaling her sweet essence, and once again I'm greeted with my slice of heaven. Desire and want take over. I have more control over my tongue than I do my cock, and at this moment, I take advantage of it. I tease her by licking straight up her center from her tight hole to the one I want my mouth in, taking her clit between my teeth and giving it a little tug, then I begin circling it slowly with my tongue. She wiggles, calls out my name, and undoes me once again. This is such a sensitive area on her, one I've grown to respect. This one little bud that God created is what sets my wife off, drives her insanely mad, takes her exactly where I love for her to go. Into motherfucking oblivion. That existence sends her hips off the bed, pressing her core further into my face. I flick it once then move to her opening, fucking it with my tongue, dictating the movements from slow to fast and deep to hard. I can't get enough of her sinful taste, and yet, outside of this room, I yield to this righteous woman whose morals overturn the wrongdoings I commit. My wife owns me.

It doesn't take long before she's coming all over my face. I inhale and lap her up until my balls ache to remind me of the fact I need to be inside her. Somehow, I manage to pull us both to the edge of the bed. Her legs are still spread, her damn body so temptingly stunning and waiting for me to take what I need.

"Fuck me, Roan." She glances up at me. That ping in my chest hits, and I take hold of her ankles, hoisting one leg up at a time, resting them on my shoulders. Her ass lifts off the bed at the perfect angle for me to drive my cock into her. I line him up and take no sympathy on fucking my woman. I pound her pussy. Every stroke in feels like I'm deeper; every stroke out makes me feel her greediness as she tries to clamp down to keep me in, to suck me dry. Never. I will never come before her.

My fingers dig into her ass, while one of her fingers goes to her clit. She's panting and moaning, while I'm thanking God for her letting me fuck this shit out of my head.

"You playing with yourself like that is going to have me coming. Christ, you are sexy as hell, woman."

She smirks. Her tiny body is bucking wildly now, her head thrashing all that wild, blonde hair into a tangled-up mess. Judging by this response from her as I screw her madly, I know she's close, and she is going to mark me with her come. But not yet. She knows the drill. I need her eyes when we come, always her eyes. It doesn't matter if I'm fucking her from behind or she's under me. I need her to know that no matter what way I take her, she sees the love I have for her when we both find that release we want.

I let her legs drop then bend to hover over her, still stroking my dick inside her, still filling her and ramming balls deep over and over until I'm fucking her from the inside out.

"Roan," she screams and compresses herself on my cock. We stare at each other. I may not be able to completely see her expression, but I have it memorized. Her eyes are half open, her mouth is slack, and she's looking at me like I'm looking at her. Like we're the only person for each other, like nothing outside of this room exists except for the life down the hall we created. My wife and I are looking at one another with pure, loyal love.

"You smell good, and you shaved." Alina rubs her hands up and down my less-bearded face, pointing out the obvious. Usually, I have a little scruff on my face. However, I hadn't shaved since before my dad's funeral, and even though she never complained last night about how rough my beard was this morning when she crawled out of bed, it sure the hell showed with the marks I left on the inside of her thighs and down her neck.

"I needed to." I glance down between her legs with a lifted brow.

"Oh, stop." She pulls away from me, walks to the table with her coffee cup in hand, and sits by Alex, who's stuffing his mouth full of toast.

I watch her interact with him for a few moments, the way she guides him thoughtfully by showing him the proper way to eat instead of shoving as much into his mouth as he can. The perfect mother and doctor that she is, she's always afraid he'll choke.

"Morning, buddy. Fist bump." I kiss the top of his head, form a fist, and knock my large one against his small one. He acknowledges me by opening his mouth wide, trying to talk. Instead, I'm greeted with that mouth full of bread with grape jelly all over it. Like the two-year-old he is, once he figures out he can't speak, he spits it out all over his plate before he gives me his toothy smile. I laugh my ass off, which causes him to laugh. Damn good kid.

"I see outside. Trucks, daddy," he mutters. There goes my heart. It flew out the window, landing right next to his big dump trucks. I glance up at Alina, who still hasn't asked me if I've found out anything. Her face shows me everything. This is all getting to her too. The being trapped inside. The normalcy gone but not forgotten.

"Not today, little man. Daddy will play trucks with you in the basement. We can play with your train too." That seems to appease him for the time being. This is the part I fucking hate. The part that makes me want to pull out my hair, scream to the holy one to ask him why. Why would you confuse and hurt an innocent child? Only, he's not the one to blame. It's the devil, good ole Lucifer himself who corrupts people to do his bidding up here while he sits on his ring of burning thrones. Stupid motherfucker.

"Talk, Roan," she demands. I glance over at her, my eyes silently pleading with her to not ask me to talk about this. Not in front of our son. He may only be two, but he picks up on the tension that's growing thicker with each passing second. Alina doesn't waver. What she does do is what any good mother would; she distracts him by reaching across the table, picking up a toy truck, and placing it in front of Alex, who forgets all about his breakfast and starts making his pretend car noises as he zooms it back and forth across his tray on his highchair.

"Calla thinks she found the man responsible. He's from the Irish," I tell her truthfully. I'm not going to tell her a damn thing about Royal, not after the hell he put her through years ago when she dated him, and sure as shit not after what he did to her before he was killed. He left scars from a hunting knife all over her body. No goddamn way am I subjecting her to relive her worst nightmare.

"The Irish. My god. Why?" Her face twists with fury, while her tone is questioning.

"I'm not sure, baby. She stopped by last night. I'm still processing the whole thing." Her features soften, while mine harden. I hate lying to her. It's a vow I gave her, but the need to protect her is stronger than that vow right now. My love for her outweighs everything. I'll do whatever it takes to protect her. Tears form in her eyes and begin to flow down her cheeks. I hate seeing her like this, so torn and worried. I reach across the table for her shaking hands. My woman, who hates this life but chose to live it because she loves me, is scared. She has every right to be, and she knows it. She may not know why Donal Sweeney killed my dad, but she knows blood will be shed, lives will be lost, and most likely, he won't stop until I kill him, or he kills me.

"I'll be safe, baby. I promise."

CALLA

I'm ignoring the icy chill filtering across my neck as Cain, Dilan, Aidan, and I sit here with my dad, who is on the brink of blowing the door wide open if these people don't hurry up. For a man with a trained eye, he sure is impatient. What can I say? I'm his daughter, and he knows, whether I'm a woman or not, I'm about to be drilled in the ass by three men right in front of him; and there isn't a thing he can do, except let me take it like I have to. This isn't sitting too well with my dad.

We're waiting on Roan and Ivan, as well as the bosses of three more families. It's do or die time for me. Today, I prove to them I can stand on my own two legs per se. I'm not worried at all. After they fire away at me like a pinball machine, we plan, we plot, and we conquer to take the Irish out, to make those bloody leeches die. It was my idea to meet here on neutral ground. This entire building is full of law offices, most of them known to be working for other families. Even though it's the middle of the night, it's the best plan I could come up with. This is the safest place we can be. I can't imagine what would happen if Donal Sweeney and his clan of fuckheads got the wind blowing in their direction and found out we were all here. I shiver thinking about it and pray none of these other families are working with him. That all of our sources and men are speaking the truth when they say they don't know a thing. Of course, the guys have spoken to them without me. They better be if they know what's good for them. They will die slowly and painfully if they are playing both sides of a one-sided coin. It's never a good idea to bet against the team who's out for revenge.

To say this feels slightly strange to be formulating and strategizing ways to execute someone when you're used to defending people in the courts of New York for crimes over half of them committed, is an understatement. It's worse than that; it's downright comical, really. Never in a million years would I have thought I would wind up where I am today when I decided to become a lawyer. With the lifestyle my parents led, you would think they would have tried to talk me out of it. Instead, Cecily and John Greer guided me to be independent.

The pure emotional strength, the obsession I strongly feel to witness this deadly game has to mean something. All the ethical, morally, or even guilty emotions can all go fuck themselves, because I'm just as much a Diamond as I am a Greer. And this man and his entire army are about ready to feel the wrath, the redemption, the absolution, and the deliverance for murdering my uncle.

It's been three days of what they call radio silence since I told Roan what I found out. Three glorious days of Cain, Justice, and myself spending every waking hour bonding, watching movies, and anything our precious child wanted to do. I thank God she still doesn't understand the concept of time, or else she would be throwing questions left and right at the two of us. Like, "Why is Daddy at home every night for dinner?" Or, "Why didn't I go to Nana and Papa's house today, while you and Daddy are working, Mommy?" It was Cain's idea to ask my parents to watch her while we both worked. When it comes to our little girl, the man trusts no one to keep an eye on her when we're not around. Overprotective is an understatement when it comes to that crazy man, and now I see why. His life is full of death, of people destroying others to the point of no return. He's fearless when he's working; he's fearful when he's not. Not even our friends can take her. It's not like she doesn't get to see all the other kids, because she does. Well, she used to anyway. Now, Aidan, Dilan, and Roan have their families locked away. If it were up to Cain, I would be living in the confines of our home as well, being heavily guarded and going out of my mind with worry while he was preparing for this. *You need to somehow find a way to get everyone together, Calla, preferably in Florida.* I make a mental note in my head to do just that while I listen to my thoughts and my dad speaking about putting a bullet through the foul-mouthed Silas Barberis, the head of the Greek Mafia, at the same time.

"You ready?" Cain grips the back of my neck, tilting my head back in his large hands to stare into my eyes, to seek out any sign of fear radiating off of me. All of a sudden, I'm nervous as hell. I guess that explains the chill I had before he put his strong hands on me.

"Of course. I can handle this, baby. It's you who needs to remember to let me do the talking. Let me answer their questions and sit there like the good little boy you're supposed to be," I say teasingly.

He smirks then brings his face down close enough for me to lick my lips and swipes his nose against mine. Oh, how I'd love to purr right now. Spread my legs and let him have me right here. If we were alone, I'd be shoved face down on this desk with my skirt wrapped around my hips and his dick reminding me we're both alive.

"I'll show you just how good of a boy I can be when we get home." Those eyes grow dark, and he lightly brushes his lips across mine.

"I bet you will." My gaze briefly travels to the growing guy in his jeans then right back to the mischievous, devilish eyes of his.

I startle at the knock on the door. Cain releases me, yet remains standing by my side with his hand on the back of my chair. How the hell

I missed knowing they were all heading up beats the shit out of me. Lost in thought, I guess.

My dad stands, his long legs striding, taking him to open the door to Roan, followed by Ivan and three men I've met briefly in passing or at functions over the past few years. I saw them all recently at my uncle's funeral. The day was a blur, and yet I remember each one of them being there, looking at the coffin with uncertainty and disbelief written all over them.

"Calla." The first man sticks his hand out for me to shake. I stand and take his hand in mine.

"Sergei," I politely say then move to shake another Russian syndicate leader's hand, otherwise known as the Petrov Bratva and allies to Ivan. He's tall, dark, handsome, and deadly. Every single man in this room has seen their share of death. Makes me feel outnumbered in more ways than being the only female daring to test the waters, to taint them.

"You look well." He kindly lifts my hand to his mouth, places a kiss across my knuckles, and takes a seat in one of the three chairs directly in front of my desk. Professional but lethal.

Next, I meet Silas Barberis, the man many people loathe; and I can see why. The Greek is a slime ball. He has his hands in everything from murder and drug trafficking to extortion and loansharking; you name it, this man has done it. Out of anyone here, he's the one I trust the least. When he places a kiss on my cheek, I can feel Cain coiling up beside me, ready to ply this notorious playboy off of me. He stands his ground though, thank God; that's all we need, my hotheaded husband to get up in this asshole's face and start a gun-slinging match in here. Half of us would be dead.

"Be prepared, Aphrodite," he whispers, instructing his psychological bullshit in my ear. The fool is trying to get a rise out of me. I know exactly what type of goddess she was. They claimed she had beauty and no brains, a loose woman. *If you only knew how much fun I want to have ripping you apart, buddy.*

"I'd say it's the other way around, Silas, wouldn't you? You see, just like her, there is more to me than meets the eye. Don't let my looks dupe you. The moment you do is the moment I strike, more like the goddess Athena." This man holds no shame. I hate him instantly, despise him to my very core. When he releases his hold on me, I cringe and shutter, for he is a man not to be trusted. I can sniff a man full of shit from a mile away. This grotesque, hair slicked back moron will do everything he can to undermine me, to try and fly under my sensor to dispose of me in ways I won't let happen. He's up to something.

I guide my gaze to my dad, whose face is pinched. There's no way he heard from across the room what Silas said, although I can tell he did not like the man touching me. I dismiss the overrated pig and train my gaze on the one man I've been waiting to meet: eighty-year-old Charley Bracco. He's American and resides in my home state of Michigan, Detroit, which is not too far from the small outskirts, where I grew up. Nor is his name unfamiliar to me. The man may be more famous in our world for surviving more bitter, bloody gang wars than any other living soul, but he's also known for his loyalty to stay out of other families' way, to strictly abide by the truces the Irish have quickly destroyed. He reminds me of my uncle and Roan. Devoted. Trustworthy. Reliable.

"You are a lucky man." He nods toward Cain before he brings me into a shaky hug.

"I am." Cain reaches across the desk to shake his hand, while I hug Ivan.

"Stay strong," he whispers into my ear. "I'm stronger than ever, now that you're here." I wink, while he rolls those mystery eyes of his. You can gain access to a person's soul through their eyes. Ivan's are always clear, always in control. Except for now. They're as dull as the rest of ours.

"Shall we begin?" Roan states. I glance at him briefly, nod, then sit up straight, folding my hands in front of me and placing them on my desk. I'm anything but prim and proper right now on the inside. I'm ruthless, unaffected, and ready to debase these men. To make them wish to God they didn't request this meeting for me to prove to them how loyal I am. I know what has to be done, and given the opportunity, I'll do it. Kill for the kill. Blood for the blood.

"I'll go first." *Of course, he will*, I think to myself when Silas speaks up, crosses his legs, and stares me down. He fails to remember I'm a lawyer who is not easily intimidated; I'll challenge this piece of shit all night long.

"I'd like to know how you plan on getting yourself out of a hostile situation, Mrs. Bexley. You're a woman, a beautiful one. There are men in this world who don't take kindly to a woman such as yourself telling them what to do. Not all of us are pulled around by a leash chained to our dicks. Are you a woman who takes risks, who will lay her life down for another? Or are you a woman who will allow a man to die for you instead? Because I'm not going to lie to you, there will come a time when not even your dad or your husband will be around to protect you." I eye him jadedly, contemplating my answer all the while envisioning my hands wrapped around his throat, squeezing until his face turns red and his eyes bulge in horror as he realizes he's sinking further into hell with no goddamn escape, because this beautiful, venomous woman is sucking the last bit of his pitiful life out of him.

Roan was right. These men do have me on trial; even Charley, as he eyeballs me with tired and aged perceptiveness waiting for my reply. I don't dare look at one single member of my family for dread these three men will think I'm weak, that I can't handle this. I can feel every single one of the men I love not making one move on the outside to show how pissed off they are or how much they want to put a bullet straight through this man's head. Especially my dad, who I know damn well is itching to cut this rancid, pox-marked creature's tongue out of his mouth and shove it up his ass.

"Hmm. Silas, those are very good questions. In fact, I should applaud you for them. But I won't. I'll tell you what I will do though. I'll kill any man out of pure entertainment who dares to cross me in a way he should not. Being a woman does not mean I can't be brutal, heartless, and meticulous. I'm the daughter of John Greer, a man who taught me how to defend myself, a man whose blood runs thick in my veins. Which means if any of you have an ounce of doubt in your mind I won't cut someone's throat simply because I'm a woman, then every single one of you better watch your back. Don't ever cross me and don't you ever come into my office and try to assume that unlike you, I will die for the ones I love, because let me set you straight; I would give my life for this syndicate. Hell, Silas, I would even give up my life for a man like you if it meant this raging war against my family would end. Either that or kill you if I had to. I may have been protected my entire life, but I'm here now. Never underestimate my power, loyalty, or love."

"Is that so?" he taunts.

I gather my thoughts as I look him square in the eyes and say, "It's very much so. I'm a woman you do not want to mess with, Silas. I answer to my counsel, my people, and I will live according to my revelation." I grit out at him while heat boils the blood in my veins and the pulse in my neck quickens as the fury of blowing this motherfucker's head off right here threatens to prove my point. I've never killed another human being before, but people can bet that just like the change of a tide, people change as well; and this bitch right here in front of them has turned cold and callous when it comes to what I will do to protect my own. I hate this fucker; he is a threat in every sense of the word. I can feel it.

"Well, I hope the time never comes for me or you to cross each other, my dear." Charley smirks, and my resolve turns to him.

"I do too, Charley." I run my tongue over my teeth, and for the next five hours, long after the sun has risen to expose itself, letting us know how excruciatingly hot it will be, I am left feeling like a detainee who has been subjected to an enhanced interrogation on my ethics, morals, and sexual humiliation; all because I'm a woman.

"I'm going to kill him." Cain's particular phrase has us all chuckling two seconds after Roan walks out the men and their dozen bodyguards, who were all standing outside of my office with guns drawn, ready to attack if things went south. He's talking about Sergei, who threw us all for a wild loop. I'm still spinning from the shock over his questions. He had my eyeballs ready to pop out of their sockets. Silas' questions were mild compared to his.

"I've never in my life had someone ask me what I would do if someone tried to have their way with me. Who asks questions like that anyway? I'm puzzled. Stumped. Thank God I didn't have to answer with Ivan and my dad's loud thundering voices screaming, "An asshole." Answering my own question before anyone else has to chance.

Roan was right. Those men tried to rape me mentally with everything they could throw my way.

It's not me they should be concerned about, for God's sake. After all, none of us would be tired and ready for bed right now if they hadn't demanded to throw their authority around. To make sure I was capable of running our empire if something were to happen to Roan. I bit my tongue several times when they asked questions a little too personal for my taste. Especially when they threw shots at my husband as if he were some kind of man I had on a string. Old school, my ass; they can't stand the fact a woman has power amongst the people, has influence and respect, or that the majority of marriages these days are equal, where a man worships his wife as much as she does him. I actually feel sorry for the women in their lives. That's as far as I'll take it though. What they do is frankly none of my concern. Unless they become involved in the defilement of a woman or kidnapping her, I couldn't care less. If that ever happens, I'm not sure what type of a person I'd turn into. A murderous one most likely.

"That's how he is; he's a sick fuck. The man is so twisted up over the fact that Calla will have more respect from others than he does, that he wanted to push her buttons to find out if he could pop one loose. When he realized he couldn't with us here, he backed down. But don't let your guard down if you're anywhere near that sick motherfucker. I'm not calling him twisted for no reason. I've seen the fucker in action. He has no value in a woman at all. Don't allow yourself to be in a situation where you're alone with him, sweetheart; he's the type of man he was talking about when he asked you what you would do if you came across a man hitting on you." I like my dad's version of his question much better than the way he asked it. The prick made it sound like it was going to happen.

"I won't ever be alone with him, Dad. I have no desire to be around a man like that. He chills me. He's a snake. I trust Silas more than I do him." His smile is small, yet it's there. He's appraising me silently with the love and pride only a father can have for his daughter. I did better than I thought I would, even though there were a few times when I honestly thought I was going to shit myself when Silas proved me to be wrong about him being a loathing creature.

I gathered myself after Sergei tried to break me down only to numb me a few questions later when he brought up the things Royal had done when he'd kidnapped Roan and me. Roan spoke up before I had the chance to register what he was saying, because flashbacks hit my brain as if someone was trying to scrub away the memories; only they were smearing them all over, making me relive the night I was drugged and lost mine and Cain's baby I hadn't known I was carrying.

"Here we all thought it was Silas who couldn't be trusted. That man is a puffed-up marshmallow compared to Sergei. And you tell me I can't watch over my wife? That motherfucker's out of line questions prove she needs me. He may be taunting her, but that motherfucker wants her. You all had your backs to him while I stood here and watched another man mentally fucking my wife. I don't care what you say; I'm not letting her out of my goddamn sight." Cain's right. There were times when I felt Sergei's eyes raking me up and down like I was sitting here naked in front of him, while I tried to barricade my mind from the delusional man.

"You're going to keep your temper in check and not gut the man the minute he looks at her. You know how this shit works, Cain. Calla is a threat to them. Female or not won't be the problem with most of the men she'll deal with. Their problem is, they are scared of her because of who she is; she's the daughter of the best contracted killer that ever existed. Every single one of them will be watching her like a hawk for fear she will kill them." I place my hand on top of Cain's to calm him down. I understand his jealousy. If a woman looked at him like she wanted to have her way with him, I would have wanted to kill her too.

"Cain, you need to stop. I love you more for wanting to protect me every second of the day, but do you really think Aidan or my dad are going to let anything happen to me? It's obvious Sergei and his crew don't respect the way we all love one another; if he did, he would have never asked that question in the first place. Besides, it's not like Roan is going to throw me into the ring with a pack of wolves and say, 'Here's your dinner, boys. Come and get it.'"

"He better fucking not," he growls.

This is when I know Cain and I need to discuss this in private before he starts to pull his hair out with the jealous rage brewing behind those irises of his. I'm the only one who's allowed to pull his hair. I give him a look, the one that says, 'Shut up. We will talk about this later.' Then I turn around and ask the one question I'm dying to know the answer to. The one that's more important than any other question slung my way tonight.

"Why didn't you bring up the Irish, Roan?"

This entire situation has my skin crawling away from my bones. Something isn't right here. Whether it's the element of being drained or the mere fact that my family is pissed off after they had to sit here and witness me being belittled and hung on the cross before I've been given the chance to prove myself. Whatever it is, I know they feel and want the answer as much as I do.

"That's the best question I've heard all night." Aidan nudges Roan with his shoulder.

"You don't trust Sergei, do you? You think he may be involved somehow?" Dilan pipes in.

"Maybe not with my dad's death, but I think that shady fucker has his hands in this underground fighting. And until Lorenzo can get inside somehow, I don't trust any of them." Roan filled me in about Lorenzo the other day. It's a brilliant idea, yet one that seems rushed to teach this young man to keep his eyes forward and his ears everywhere. He then called everyone else to let them know about this young kid. We all agreed this is the only option we have in this short period of time.

My eyes go wide. I knew it had something to do with not trusting Sergei, but surely he can trust Charley. The man is commonly known to be as faithful as we are.

"Do you trust the others?" I ask, my question filled with trepidation. My spine is tingling and straightening at the same time. What the hell is Roan not telling us? What did he mean by not trusting any of them? Questions are piling up, and I don't have the answers to a single one of them. Calmly, Roan swipes his hands down his weary face. I'll admit, when he first showed up tonight, he looked a hell of a lot better than the last time I'd seen him. He appears to be rested, more alert, but it's the cool way he composes himself like he's protecting all of us that scares the hell out of me. It's the way he's transfixed on my dad and Ivan as if they know what's going on too. It's the way he looks at his brothers, who are as shocked at his levelheaded demeanor as I am. My heart leaps around in my chest. My soul is telling me this isn't good. Roan has information he's not ready to share, something big, and I have the nagging feeling it has everything to do with why he really didn't bring up our suspicions tonight. Trust may be a fraction of his reason, but what he has to say is the real truth as to why.

"Something tells me I can trust Silas. I don't think he was trying to break you. I believe he was going to bat for you by letting you prove how strong you are. And Charley," he shrugs. "He's too old to start shit," Roan answers truthfully. I sigh in relief. Except he's still holding back his reason for not sharing our suspicions.

"Tell them." My dad's deep and heavy comment hangs heavy in the air. I begin to sweat underneath my silk shirt. My mind is racing to figure out what he could have discovered, what he seems to be bitterly nervous to tell us. When he finally discloses his information, all the air leaves my lungs along with the hot, sticky sweat dripping down my back. A cold rush seeps into my veins, freezing me on the spot. The only part of me left untouched from the bitter frost of his words is my brain trying to wrap its way around what he said.

"Someone burned down the club in Michigan. Priscilla and Bronzer are dead."

ROAN

"What?" Cain whispers as I watch his face morph from anger to disbelief and heartache. Tasting the anguish and despair in this room is worse than receiving the phone call from a detective back in Detroit, who helped keep an eye on the club we all loved. Our hangout, Cain's home, and everything he's fought for to turn that club around are gone. Innocent people were most likely tortured in ways they've only heard about before the soulless motherfuckers stole their lives. It's another dose from those that have snuck out of nowhere to make us submit, to try and dominate over my empire. To reduce my family to nothing. Instead of facing me with their vendetta, they seem to think I owe. They take the coward's way and have stricken us once again with the only weapon they have: to brutally murder those we love.

Cain's club, the one he turned around from the devious, deceitful father of his, who'd blackballed us all into thinking it was good, when behind Cain's back, he had his hands in some fucked-up, shady shit that ended up claiming his life in the end, leaving his only son to pick up the pieces. It was a goddamn mess of a place until Cain pulled his head out of his ass and straightened it out, turned it away from drugs, yet kept our lives hidden. Of course, the majority of them knew what we did and who we were, but it never once stopped them from loving us, welcoming all of us back with arms wide open when we'd go to visit. Hell, they closed the place down for a long weekend and came to my wedding.

Priscilla and Bronzer paid the price for revenge with their lives. For years, we've kept our old stomping grounds neutral to keep them as far away from our lives here as possible. Kept them safe. Cain and Calla visited there often. Fuck, he even built a home for the two of them there before they got back together, and now it's gone. Burned to the fucking ground. Rubble. Ashes. With the remains of a husband and wife in the mix of it.

"Why the fuck didn't someone tell me or have the decency to call me? That was my club. My home. Priscilla was… Christ, she was my goddamn sanity for years when I cleaned that place up. She was like a sister to me, and now she's dead alongside her husband. What the fuck, Roan?" I let Cain fight his pain as we all stand there and deal with our own. I've had time since this morning to compact all this in my brain and watch it drain down to my heart and drown the hell out of me. Thank God for an understanding, sympathetic wife, because there is no damn way I can take another step without that strong woman holding my hand. I'm not afraid to scream that shit to the world. I need her in order to breathe. She's the one who made me promise to wait until this meeting was over to tell them, for fear Calla would stumble, not have her mind where it should be. It destroyed me not to tell them. But I had to do what was right. Cain knows this, and even though I see it the minute his eyes reflect back to mine, I'm telling him like it is anyway. I love the man, but he has the quickest temper when he feels backed into a corner. He needs to hear my reason why, whether he wants to or not. They all do, for that matter.

"I feel your betrayal, brother. Detective Branch called me shortly before I left the house. They have evidence to believe it was the Irish." Cain goes to speak, stumbling over the words he can't seem to get out. His hands are gripping the side of the desk to support his wavering balance. I continue telling them what they need to hear before I shove a dagger straight through their hearts. "There was no way I was bringing it up before those men got here. They would have eaten her alive, and you know it. She would be the laughing stock before our feet even step outside of this building. If there is one thing I can say about any of us, it's that we love each other. When one hurts, we all hurt. On top of that, you would have killed Sergei ought of spite and anger for those who killed our friends. I needed Calla focused. As far as them not calling you instead of me, I called Branch shortly after the funeral, told him about my dad and to keep an extra watch on the place, just in case whoever the hell did this decided to strike us there." By the look on Cain's face, brows furrowed, tears in his eyes, he understands why they called me instead of him. Doesn't mean shit when two wonderful people we all love have lost their lives because of me and some sick bastard who's out for revenge. I've never felt so guilty for breathing when someone else isn't in all my life. It's a nightmare on repeat. One I know will return when I close my eyes tonight from the sleeping pill Alina will place in my hand. People are being killed because of me. The fucked-up part is, I have no clue why. Why this fucker is attacking me, making me and those I love suffer when I haven't done a damn thing to him. I'm about to though. I'm about to fuck his world, one finger and toe at a time until I feel I've avenged the murder of my loved ones. Even then it won't be enough. How anyone could take the life of an innocent person is beyond me.

"You're sure this is the work of the Irish?" I narrow my eyes at Aiden, who loved the two of them as much as Cain and I did.

"I'm fucking positive."

"And how's that? Did someone actually witness it, report to the cops what they saw? I mean, fuck, Roan, the club used to have enemies. Cain's dad wasn't a goddamn saint." Aidan points out something we already know. Anger burns inside of me at the thought of Cain's dad. However, the proof was left behind. Proof that's going to rip apart whatever sense of reality my family has when I tell them. No matter what I do or say, I cannot save them from this. I study them all; their reactions to this news are pure shock. John has his back to me. His chest is heaving up and down in anger even though I already told him. The news was shocking enough to me; I needed to get it off my chest to someone besides Alina. He was the first person I thought of calling. Then I called Ivan. I needed his guidance, because frankly, my mind is fucked up. I'm hanging loosely here. I look over to Calla, who has tears in her eyes and her arms wrapped around Cain as she buries her head in his chest. Aidan is on the verge of tears. The only one who is looking at me with a hate-filled expression is Dilan. He didn't know them, but he knew of them. He knew we loved them and what that place meant to all of us.

"By these." I reach into the inside of my suit jacket and pull out the photos Detective Branch couriered to me after he called.

"Motherfucking dead men!" Cain yells loud enough to make Calla jump as every single one of them stares down at the two photos on top of her desk.

"Oh my God. No!" Calla places her head as far into Cain's chest as she can, her cries wailing. The strong woman from minutes ago is gone. All that's left is a shell that's been ripped wide the fuck open. The rest of us stare with the look of horror at this human we loved, his body placed like some damn trophy to these sick fucks. One of the photos has bottles of the Black Bush Irish Whiskey lined up along the gate of the club. Green paper four-leaf clovers are scattered all over the place.

I feel like someone shoved their hand down my throat, wrapped their slimy fingers around my heart, and yanked it out, leaving me as heartless as I feel.

The other photo has four smaller ones all from different angles of Bronzer slumped on the floor in front of the main bar at the club. His dead eyes are burning a hole in our memory as he stares back at us in shock, the evidence stuck right between his chest: a pocket knife with the Celtic sign etched into the wooden handle. The sign of the Irish. Donal left behind a message this time when he killed innocent people. The people we love. Either he knows we have him figured out, or whatever sick, twisted plan he derived with my dead brother has only begun.

"Go get the young man now, Roan." It's as if my dad has spoken when we all gladly tear our gazes away from a sight I never want to see again, to the deadly, fearless eyes of my father-in-law.

"You mean Lorenzo?" I say, knowing that's whom he means. All of us do in this room. We all agreed this is the only option we have. Time isn't on our side, now more so after what happened to our friends.

"Yes. He has one week to train, to learn, and to see if he has the balls to kill if he needs to or no balls at all."

"Damn, that has to hurt," I tell Dilan while we stand with Lenny, watching his son spar at the gym he trains at, or more like pummel his partner into the mat with every blow to the dude's face. Headgear on or not, the guy has to be hurting.

After we all had left the meeting where Calla took all three men down with her confidence and masterful words that left them wobbling out of her office with their dicks shoved in their mouths, then my hurtful message that destroyed her along with everyone else, Cain and Calla went home to get some rest. They're both going to need it, since we have to move fast. "None of us can take a chance on losing any more of the people we love." Those were Ivan's words as we left the building, despondent, to say the least. Every one of us has a role to play. Aidan is making arrangements for a proper burial for our friends who lost their lives because of some sick revenge I'm still trying to figure out. John went home to spend time with Aunt Cecily and Justice, because he knows he's coming out of retirement. I fucking need him in more ways than I can count. The most important part being, my uncle has a soul when it comes to his family. He lives and breathes us all, but when it comes to killing someone, he turns into an unrecognizable man. A robot with no heart. A human trained to kill and maim you. To make you wish to God you were dead. A destroyer whose brain takes over with the desire to kill to match the crime. No one really knows the ways he chooses to snuff the life out of someone; all I know for sure is, there isn't a trace left behind when he is done. Another thing I know is, every damn one of them will suffer before they die. Brutally.

If I could change one thing from tonight, it would have been to tell Calla she outsmarted every man in there. I'm proud of the way she handled herself today; she proved even more that she can handle whatever is thrown her way. Especially with the words and lack of respect Sergei spewed at her. That man has me on edge by the way he tried to break her. If he is up to something, he sure didn't give two fucks to try and hide it. Either that or he wants her, which will never happen. He tries to look her way just once, and I will give any one of my men the orders to first cut out his tongue then kill him anyway he sees fit. Sick bastard. I wish I could have crushed his windpipe right there. He's all sorts of fucked up. I make a mental note to tell her how well she did the first chance I get at the same time paying attention to a young kid who hits his target with punches and kicks like he wants to kill him.

"Enough, gentlemen. Lorenzo, come down here." The two men stop. The one I know to be Lorenzo spits out his mouthguard, unfastens his headgear, tossing it to the ground, then reaches down and helps the guy he beat the shit out of up off the floor. Why the hell anyone would want to let someone wail the hell out of them like he just did is beyond me.

I'm a baseball man; boxing, ring fighting, and all this beating on each other until your opponent is half dead is a sport I know little about. That's beside the point. What we're here for is to find out if this young man is willing to pay the price to get inside for us. To go incognito and hope like hell Donal has no idea his father works for me.

"Son, these are Roan Diamond and his cousin Dilan Levy." Lenny introduces us with pride dripping from his words and the look that only a father has when he's introducing his child. Love, adoration, and importance. This young kid means everything to him. I've seen this look many times coming from my dad. Jealousy courses through my veins, and my dad's face appears in my vision as I watch Lenny grab his boy by the back of the neck, giving him that fatherly squeeze, letting him know how proud he is of him. As crazy as it sounds, I also envision Alex and me like this someday. Then that shit called reality sucker punches me again, knowing my son can only grow up with me by his side if I live through this war. I grew up with both of my parents putting both my older brother and me first until he betrayed us and wound up dead. I can't let that happen to my child or any other children Alina and I will be blessed with. Especially this young man who's willing to sacrifice his life by rolling right into the pits of hell. He'll be committing suicide if he's caught and then breaks down from their torture they will inflict on him. I must lead this war to protect him and all the other members of our family. Times like these make me wonder if I have it in me to continue with this legacy. To put the syndicate before those I love, and fight to the death for them. The kind of man Dad has never forced me to be. He gave me that choice. He might have been disappointed if I'd walked a different path; he may have handed it down to someone else, but he would have never tried to force me. No. I've made the decision years ago to carry on being a criminal with morals and ethics, if that makes sense. Which, really, it doesn't, but it's the truth.

"Good to meet you, man." Dilan sticks out his hand for him to shake, his voice bringing me back to the man I need to focus on. I swing my eyes the young man's way. He shows no fear, no lack of confidence with his strong grip, his eye contact that lets me know Lenny has already spoken to him.

"You're a brave man for agreeing to do this. It's a situation not many would agree to be thrown into. I need to know I can trust you. Lives will be at stake here, including yours if this isn't played out right. They are to know nothing about me, nothing about you. Your name will be erased. You will have a new identity, no contact with your family or girlfriend, only with Dilan or me until we say otherwise. You're going in blind, all on your own. You need to understand that before we begin to plan, Lorenzo, because if you don't, it will be you we bury next." He's a brave motherfucker by the way he doesn't bat a lash at my blunt words and shows no fear, no urgency or miscommunication when I tell him the truth. He's going in as the enemy, a new fighter; he may have to kill, and one slip of the tongue could get him killed if they find out who he is.

"I understand completely, Roan. Trust me when I say they have no clue who I am or who my father is. I'm one of the thousands of men who trains at a gym. I don't have a girlfriend for us to worry about. If I did, I wouldn't be doing this. I also want revenge on the people who killed a man my father loved. I may have been shielded and protected from the syndicate, but I'm not oblivious. I know the kind of shit that goes down. You have my word I'm not afraid to bring this fucker's house to the ground." I hear him clearly, the way he speaks with confidence. What I need to know is if he truly does understand what he's about to step into. Donal is a man motivated by power and control. His one goal is to expand his empire. Like the rest of us, he plots, waits, and always has the bigger picture in mind. To get ahead; and to be ruthless in doing so. The difference between the way he works and the way we do is, we don't sacrifice the ones we love to manipulate them into a desperate position, where the only choice you have is to live or die. I may not be manipulating Lorenzo; this is a decision I have no doubt he made with his father, who also knows his son is in danger. What I am doing is throwing him into the cage with an animal that's as dangerous as one with rabies. Full of madness and with a fatal bite.

"I need a trainer to go in with me," Lorenzo tells us after we've had the dreaded discussion. This man is a powerhouse. His size alone can intimidate a stranger walking down the street. I thought I was buff. Shit, I'm a weasel compared to the build on Lorenzo. He's a bulky motherfucker who towers over the top of me.

I turn my gaze just as I hear Dilan say, "I hear you, man. Let us handle the technicalities, you stayed focused." I know in an instant who will be all over this shit.

"Lorenzo," I say, interrupting the two of them. "We need someone in there who knows what they are doing, someone I trust. I need to make sure whoever is in there with you has no problem killing someone if they have to. Do you get me?"

"I get you, Roan."

"Good." I nod. I know just the guy who will do it, but first I need to make sure Lenny is okay with this too. He may have volunteered his son to be our eyes and ears underground, but has he thought this through, knowing the possibilities? It's obvious Lenny has spoken with him in great lengths about this. I should be telling Dilan to get on the phone and call Jackson's brother, and yet at this moment, I'm gauging Lenny's reaction, watching tediously to make sure our trusted family friend is truly okay with what his son is about to do.

"You sure about this, Lenny? You know damn well I'll find another way in there. I hate keeping him from you and the rest of your family. But I don't have a choice; it's for everyone's protection, especially his." He looks at his son for a long, tender moment, then nods his head, an easy smile forming on his lips.

"Just like your father with you, I've not once forced my son to do something he wasn't comfortable doing. When I told you the other day about him being your guy, that wasn't me talking, Roan, that was him.

He knows I'm hurting in here," he points to his chest, even though that hurt and pain is plain to see as it's seeped out of his chest and onto his features. "He wanted revenge before I brought this up to him. No matter what I feel, I believe in my son as your father believed in you. He has a good head on his shoulders. Now, all you need to do is train him to use it in the way of your world. Train him to not only kill with his hands but to gut every bastard who crosses their eyes at him. I trust you with his life. If I didn't, none of us would be standing here." I perceive him, hear him, and above all else, promise him I will keep his son safe. He knows as well as I do that's a promise I'm not sure I can keep.

CALLA

"You going to be all right, baby?" Cain asks when we arrive home to an empty house. I'd be a hell of a lot better if our daughter were here with us so I could hold her, see her smiling face, listen to her giggle, watch her and Cain play with her dolls. That's the thing about having a child; they can make all your worries go away with just one look, touch, or the mere innocence that radiates off them like a bright flashing beam of light. A rainbow full of colors.

It took all I had not to tell my dad to bring her home instead of letting her spend the rest of the day with them. He would have done it, no questions asked. I just couldn't, not with what has happened, or what's yet to come. He deserves to spend time with her, even if it's for reasons she will hopefully never understand, not until she's older anyway. I sigh, not prepared at all to think of the repercussions that could come back to my entire family once Justice is old enough to know who her parents, grandparents, and the rest of her family are. I can't think of any of that right now. I need to stay focused on the here, the now, and what the next week will bring us. More death, more blood, and more heartache.

Cain nor I have barely said a word to one another since we left the office I never want to go back to. Too much bad shit has been seen, spoken, and delivered to me in that god-forsaken place, that if I never have to step through those doors again, it won't be enough to erase any of that. I can't get those visions out of my head. You would think I could handle it after the many marred or beaten photos of dead people I've seen over the years of being a lawyer. Not one of them were members of my family or friends though, not like the friends we lost. The friends whose faces will be forever embedded in my brain so much it physically hurts everywhere, knowing I will never see them again.

And believe me, I have seen some terrible things. Except, they were villains themselves, men who betrayed, became disloyal, men who deserved it. But this, seeing innocent people murdered, knowing those bastards killed a woman when anyone in their right mind knows that taking the life of a woman or a child is a goddamn living sin makes me want to blow their heads off. Only one woman I knew of deserved that kind of treatment: Jazmin Carlos; the bitch she was is dead and living in hell by Roan's hand. She got what was coming to her; her head was blown off her body for the things she did to Anna and Dilan. Sick, twisted shit that made her deserve to die. Not a woman as kind, sweet, and innocent as Priscilla. My god, how terrified she must have been. The only thing I can hope for is that she wasn't tortured before they killed her. Oh God, that thought makes me want to vomit.

"What if they tortured her, or worse yet…" I turn to Cain, the pain in his eyes reflecting my own. I'm unable to say the word that's stuck on the edge of my tongue. I need some kind of proof, proof I'll never get that they didn't hurt her in that way.

My fingers twitch at the thought. I've never killed anyone. The way I feel right now though, I'm ready to strike people dead.

"Calla, we can't think that way. The what ifs will destroy us. All we can do is take this time to grieve for them. To remember them as the people they were. You're hurting; I'm hurting. We'll get through this together." His words are soft, warm, and tender. I know him; he desperately wants to lash out. To lose control. Roan was right when he talked about Cain's temper earlier; he's quick to fly off the handle, speak his mind. Now he contains it for me. I'm not sure if I want him to let loose, to go to the basement and pound on his punching bag until his knuckles bleed, or if I want him to fuck me like a madman right now. All I do know is, I need to be in his big, strong arms.

He must know what we both need when I feel his breath hit my lungs, sucking mine right into his when he lunges for me, pulls me into him, and devours my mouth with his. Furiously. This is crazy, the two of us pawing away at each other while two people who loved, cherished, and spoke those sacred marriage vows will never be able to consume one another like this again. I feel sick over it, yet I'm incapable of stopping. I need him as much as he needs me. It's an addiction no one has been able to cure; it's normal to want that connection with the one you love when life has tilted your world into a spiraling, out of control mess. You do it to survive the chaos while clinging to the one you love. And… God, I love Cain with everything I have. I've loved him since I was sixteen years old.

Our teeth clash; we bite each other with a frantic recklessness that has me gasping for air. His hands are digging into the flesh of my ass when he lifts me up and backs me up against the wall in the hallway.

"Goddamn, I want to take you hard, sink my cock into your body, and then pound you into this wall." It's been a long time since he's taken me like this. A child sneaking out of her bedroom at night tends to leave you limited with where you can screw your husband. Not that we don't use every resource we have in our room or take advantage of times like these when Justice is gone. We do, all the time. Not that we mind the middle of the night sex either. I'll take this pleasurable man any chance

I can get, because doing exactly what we're about to do is what gave her to us.

"Do it. Don't hold back. Fuck me," I gasp, barely able to stand it. He attacks my neck, sucking, biting, and hitting the spot, driving an aching sensation right to the center of my body, the one place I want my husband: my throbbing pussy.

"Jesus Christ, Calla, I can feel the heat off of you through our clothes. Take them off now. All of them." Damn, I'm smacked with a dose of déjà vu of when I first came back to the States all those years ago with the way he bosses me around as if he owns me. He was bossy back then. Today, he's downright domineering. Our marriage is equal in every way, but when Cain wants something as much as he wants me, he turns into a dominating man, after one thing, and all I can do is submit, surrender, and let him take control. It's been a long time since this side of him has evolved into the side of him I've craved. I need to be fucked.

My fingers shake as I make quick work of my clothes and shoes, stopping mid-stride when his glorious cock springs free from his jeans, showing me the perfect view of the lily tattoo down the length of those inches that split me wide, control my body, and send me into a galaxy all our own every time he enters me.

"Good God in heaven, it's only been a few days since I've felt you, Cain. It's been way too long since I've seen you in daylight. You are a gift. If you don't fuck me, I'll be forced to drop to my knees to get my taste of you."

A low, pleasured moan comes out of his mouth; then he says what any woman wants to hear when she needs her man between her thighs. "Don't worry, babe, I'm going to fuck you until you scream, slam into you until you're dripping wet and coming all over my cock, then I'm burying myself balls deep while my cum fills your tight pussy."

"That filthy mouth of yours could make me come right now," I say and pull my jeans the rest of the way off, not once taking my eyes off of that tattoo, the representation of my name. Over the past few years, he's gotten a few more too. One arm is completely covered with some brotherly tribal design on his shoulder and upper arm that Deidre drew up for all the guys, a colorful design of swirls so intricately detailed on his lower arm you don't know where the beginning or end is. It's beautiful; it's him.

He glances up and down my naked body, admiring my breasts, stomach, legs, and then landing on my bare pussy before he speaks.

"You fucking love my filthy mouth, especially when it's buried between those thighs. If you're going to come before I get in there, then by all means, come; but do it on my face," he challenges. The snarly bastard. "Now, I hope for your sake you're ready for me, cause you're about to be fucked with nine inches of a cock that wants inside of its master." His gaze is probing my mouth. The need to come back with some smartass retort is ready to fly off the tip of my tongue. Instead, I smirk. His brows lift, surveying my expression.

"I was just thinking how I always submit to whatever you want when you go all badass and demand me to be ready for you, then you turn around and call my pussy your master." I can't help but laugh. Cain doesn't find it funny though, which makes me laugh harder.

"Fucking mine. Always mine." He slides his index finger down my center. My laughter subsides instantly. The man teases my clit with one swirl, then tugs it hard enough to make me gasp. "I'll be your slave, your lover, your best friend, your equal, and your every damn thing for the rest of my life, Calla. You submit; I submit. You play master; I play master. I don't care, as long as it's with you, I'll do whatever the hell you want." He keeps his hand over the top of my core in the possessive way he always touches me as if he still can't believe we're together. His eyes are drilling his love for me into the bottomless depths of my soul.

"I love you, Cain, but please, fuck me." His words are sweet. I'm not in the mood for sweet right now. Not when I know how this man can fuck.

He hoists me up, not once taking those eyes that drown out any worries or misfortunes off of mine. My legs wrap around him, and I press the heels of my feet into the firmness of his ass.

I buck wildly against him when he slams himself into me, the feeling of being filled with him sending my head backward, banging against the wall.

"Ah fuck. You grip me so damn tight," he bellows out. My mind is somewhere in the clouds, my back is arched, and before I know it, my husband's hands are squeezing my ass as he pummels his dick inside of me. I can't speak; the pleasure is too much, too intense, too primal. It's raw.

"You love it when I ram my cock into you like this. So wet and tight. You can't get enough; you want my cum in this tight little cunt, don't you, baby? You wanted it, now take it," he grunts. That damn talk of his sends me straight to the edge, where I stand still before plummeting into a downward spiral, riding out my orgasm. Cain drills, he swears, he hits every spot he possibly can, while my head knocks against the wall, my breasts bounce, and my body is being thoroughly programmed to take his rough fucking, his overbearing stare. Repeatedly.

"I'm coming, baby. Come with me." And I do. I tighten my grip on him, sparks flying around us as we come together. He's buried like he said he would be. His warmth is seeping inside of me.

"Christ. I love you so much. Don't go anywhere, Calla. Never leave me. I swear to God as my witness, I won't survive without you." In the blink of an eye, my badass is gone. In his place returns the grief-stricken leader, friend, and confidant. He's struggling to hold it together, fighting off tears that want to fall if only to help him ease his pain, to let it out and be human. Even a man can cry. They too can wear manifestations on their sleeves, to not be ashamed to show a side they keep hidden. It kills me, breaks my heart to see him struggle internally with losing two people who meant the world to him.

"Let it go, Cain," I speak softly. My hands move from the tight grip they have around his neck to hold his face. He's still buried inside of me when he walks us down the hall to our room, but slips out of me before allowing me to glide down his body. No words are spoken. None need to be. He drags the covers open for me to slide into. It isn't until he pulls me close to him that he lets loose and cries.

~

"You clean your plate, little girl, then you can have one of Nana's brownies," Cain scolds Justice at the dinner table. She can get away with about anything with him but this. He's a slave driver when it comes to making sure she eats her food, takes her vitamins, and brushes her teeth. The rest, he usually leaves up to me. I watch her pout, cross her arms over her chest, and puff the strands of her dark hair out of her face, then turn back to my mom, who's helping me clean up the kitchen. Cain and I slept for three hours before we caved and called my parents. Now, here we are after they brought her home an hour later along with everything to make tacos. On any given day, those are Justice's favorite. I'm not sure why she's acting like a little stinker by not eating.

"Kids are resilient in some ways and observant in others, honey. She was full of questions today," Mom tells me.

"Like what?" I say, my voice low, my tone full of concern.

"Mostly about why she can't go outside, why she can't ride her bike." That is the moment my heart literally can't take any more.

"What did you tell her?" I whisper. Guilt is sinking into the holes of my gaping heart. "God, Mom, I thought she was doing okay, that she accepted our reasons. Clearly, she isn't."

"I told her you and Cain have been busy at work, that you would take her somewhere special to ride her bike as soon as you could." I look at my mother, really look at her. We are so much alike in many ways and so very different in others. The way we can lie easily to protect those we care about. She has no idea how long this could go on. Hell, after everything that's happened, I'll be surprised if Cain doesn't get some crazy notion in his head, like when she does have the chance to go outside, she'll be attached to his body with a chain, body armor, and God knows what else to protect her. *I'm sorry, baby girl, that I chose a crazy man to be your father.* Of course, I don't mean those irrational words running through my mind.

"It's the best and the scariest feeling in the world to be a mother. You're a good one, my beautiful girl. I'm not going to get all sappy, not with those adorable little ears sitting over there while she's finally eating. I will say this; you're a brave woman, Calla. The job Roan has could have been mine if I hadn't given it up to give my daughter a life. I want you to know, my childhood was wonderful in spite of who my parents were. They loved both Salvatore and me more than anything. Back then, women didn't have a choice. They stood by their husband's side, were left in the dark about a lot of things. My mother hated the fact I was like my father, that the need to be involved with the family business was etched in my blood. Just like yours. I hate this for you. So does your dad. You dove in with both feet, created your stamp in this life. You will be a great second-in-command, Calla." I lean my head on her shoulder, her confidence in me sealed tightly in my chest.

"As far as being a mother goes, you, as her mom, will always worry every time she steps out of this door. It's human nature, unconditional love. No matter how old your child or children are, you will worry." Her words are comforting in some ways, scary in others. This isn't something the two of us hadn't discussed in great detail before I made the choice to do right by my family. Both Cain and I thought of Justice first and what this would all mean for her. It was a decision I thought through thoroughly. I knew deep in my heart she would always be protected. It's the sheltered part I will always worry about for the rest of my life. I also worry what this will mean for her when she's old enough to understand. Will she be like my mother and give it up herself? Or will she become like my dad and me, wanting to serve her family? To be pulled in every direction to protect those she loves? It truly is the scariest feeling in the world. The scariest part of it all is, once you commit to a life in the syndicate, there's no way out anymore. Not like there used to be. My mother may have been able to stop doing what she did; my father did not. No matter how I look at it, my daughter will always be in danger.

ROAN

I've never been more thankful for having a crooked cop as well as a private investigator in my back pocket than I do right now. I trust very few of those fuckers. These two, my dad trusted with his life. I used to ask him how in the hell he could trust a cop who'd pledged an oath to put people like us behind bars, and a damn investigator who worked for them. His reply was always the same. "Only the people I trust with my life know Hector Moran is my father's illegitimate son, Roan. You know this. He's my brother. For everyone's protection, especially his, we promised each other we would never speak a word about it. We also promised each other that no matter what the cost, if something were to happen to either one of us, the other would do everything in their power to help our families out. I trust him. As far as a cop. Eh," He waved his hand in the air as if to brush the sound of the word 'cop' out of his office. "We all have them in our back pockets." Dad was always good at being blunt when it came to business, saying what he had to say, nothing more, and nothing less. "A busy man doesn't dawdle on repeating himself. A trustworthy man doesn't need words repeated. You always remember that, son." I hadn't quite understood that phrase until now. It means you say what you have to say, and if the person you are speaking to is trustful, they understand you the first time. They do what must be done.

I met in private with Stauffer last night, the cop my dad had trusted. Lenny drove us around the outskirts of New York for hours while we derived a plan. I need a safe place for Lorenzo to move into, one that looks like he's been living there for a while, and I need one for Jackson's brother, Jeremy, too. Jeremy, the man they call 'The Sandman.' He runs a gym upstate. He's too old to be in the ring with these young men; my alternative plan is much better. I needed him to agree to train Lorenzo, and agree he did without hesitation. The man went as legit as he could after seven years in prison for manslaughter. The man he killed, Nathan Squires, raped and killed Sandman's wife. Sandman went ballistic, found the fucker, and choked him to death in one of those chokehold-fighting techniques. He was sentenced to six to twenty for premeditated murder. Got out on good behavior, or so they say. I'm sure my dad had his hands in helping him get out early shortly after Jackson was killed years ago. He came to Jackson and his woman's funeral, who were both brutally murdered. Jeremy's hands and feet were shackled, and he had a guard in tow. He stood stoic, expressionless. I felt his stare behind the rims of my sunglasses, the need, and the desire to kill infiltrating through his veins. They hauled his ass right back after we stood like statues, watching them lower their caskets in the ground. Jeremy never spoke a word. He didn't need to; he had the look of seeking retaliation all over him. He was out two months later. So now, I have Sandman getting his shit together to move down here and train a few weeks with Lorenzo before they get him on a card for fight night.

As far as Hector goes, I haven't spoken to him much since the funeral, but I do need him for backup protection on the night Lorenzo can and will finally get into a cage with one of the Irish. For now, the call to him can wait.

My mind is drifting back to my dad, wondering if he would agree with the way I'm going about things, when I raise my head to my wife standing in the doorway. She's all the medicine I need to erase the guilt that's suffocating the fuck out of me from every angle.

"I'm thinking about giving notice to the hospital," Alina tells me after the restless night's sleep I've had, not to mention all the other shit I have going on. Her calmness before the storm of her statement should soothe me. Instead, it has me raging like the ocean floor right before a tsunami is about to strike. She has hit me out of nowhere with this.

"Why the hell would you do that?" I ask her. She strides casually into my office at our home, still in her sexy little t-shirt. Her hair is still messed up from sleeping; her eyes are shining brightly. My wife is up to something as she cautiously makes her way to me, pushes herself up on my desk, and places a foot on my chair, right between my legs, spinning me to face her.

My blood is erupting in my veins; it doesn't stop my dick from instantly going hard though. I'm pissed off at this entire situation. If this has anything to do with the fact she is unable to leave here for the time being, I'm going to not only flip my shit but say I don't give a fuck what the hell happens; I will find the motherfucker who put my wife in this position and kill him.

I have more shit to deal with, and now she wants to bog me down with this when she knows damn well I would put whatever is troubling her first. Except, here's the thing: she doesn't look troubled at all; she looks relieved, which further ups my infatuation with this crazy shit she's talking about. "Alina, you love your job; up until we had Alex, you breathed it."

"I still love my job, baby; it has nothing to do with that." She's stalling, toying with me.

The only time she wasn't excited to go back to work was when her maternity leave was up, like most mothers, I suppose. Thankfully, the hospital has a daycare center for employees. It's expensive as hell, but at least she could see him when she had the chance; and he was safe, which was a big issue for her. That right there was more important than anything. And now, well fuck, none of us are safe. I lean back in my chair and study her composure. Her face doesn't give away a thing. Her eyes do though, as they skim down my body and land directly on my cock. What the hell is she up to?

Fuck me when her eyes take a leisurely stroll back up by body and latch onto mine with that sultry look like she wants to fuck the hell out of me. This blonde-haired temptress has my nerves simmering, my cock on fire for her, and now I know she has something stewing in that sexy little head of hers by the way her sexual pull has me gravitating to the way she tilts her head and places a foot on each arm of my chair, her long legs spreading wide, her lace-covered pussy right there for me to admire. She better spit it out, or she's going to lose the control she has over me. I'm this close to bending her over my desk and fucking some sense into her.

"Are you trying to stir my primitive emotions, Alina? Or," I grab her legs, tugging her ass to the edge. Her breath hitches the higher up my jumpy, throbbing fingers go. Fuck, I can already taste her. Sweet and sinful.

"Are you trying to use this body to get me to agree with you quitting your job?" Goddamn, she is gorgeous. She can quit her job if this is what she wants. Not at the expense of me. My wife ran away from this life before I met her, lived through hell for years with no contact with her parents because of her decisions. They let her go so she could become who she wanted to be, one of the best pediatricians in this state. They left her alone, kept her safe while she studied to be a doctor in England, all because they loved her.

She returned home for a job she loves and to a nightmare with my brother, who was obsessed with her in an unhealthy way. She became a pawn in my revenge to kill that crazy, motherfucking brother of mine.

One look from her changed it all for me. I fell in love with her before our first date, first kiss, first everything. I knew she had to be mine. I'm still falling for her, every day. This beautiful woman, who escaped the syndicate world of murder, corruption, and evil, came back to it for me. She will not give up her dream for it.

"Now, what gives you that idea, Roan?" She smirks, then skims her fingers down my chest.

"You're playing with fire, woman. Spill it. Why the hell do you want to quit doing what you love?" My ears perk up waiting on her reply. At first, she says nothing, her eyes jaunting vicariously over my facial features.

"I'm pregnant, Roan." Now my ears are straining to wonder if they heard her right.

"You are?" I ask, enthusiastically. My fingers skip wanting to delve into her tightness and move straight to her stomach. Damn. We're having another baby. My god. I'm happy as any man can be when he finds out the woman he loves is having his baby, except all I can see is my dad's face as I remember how excited and thrilled he was when we told him Alina was pregnant with Alex. You wouldn't have known he was the leader of a group of criminals. A man who had a lot of blood on his hands. No, my dad was ready to buy up the damn store with every kid toy he could find. When Alex was born, he threw his authority around, demanding he held him before anyone else in our family did. And now, he's not here to celebrate this with me. The good news she's telling me causing the tears that sting my eyes.

"Hey, are you okay?" I close my eyes at the sound of her delicate voice. My heart is disintegrating instantly when I spot the unshed tears in her eyes. She knows.

I smirk and cup her face like I've done many times when I need her to listen, because the words I want her to hear hold nothing short of the truth.

"I will be. God, beautiful lady, I'm so in love with you. There isn't a thing you could do to make me stop. Our little creation," I lean down and kiss her still flat belly. "Alex, our life is what I live for. Nothing means more to me than what we have. I'm happy we're having another baby. You are simply stunning when you're pregnant. I'm more than okay. It's just…" I can't bring myself to say it. I've thought it, know it, and yet right now, the words are a nasty taste in my mouth, ones that shouldn't be in my thoughts when my wife is telling me we're having another child.

"You miss him," she whispers. God, she knows me so well, sometimes better than I know myself. This is what I should be thankful for, the fact my dad loved her, accepted her and her family into ours, knowing at first they were rivals in this polluted world of crime, where we were both on opposites ends of the spectrum. Love, honor, and loyalty brought our families together. Now our children, the next generation of the Diamond Empire, will rule alongside their cousins, the Solokovs, if they choose.

"More than I can bear sometimes. I fall asleep thinking of him. I wake in the morning expecting his call, then I realize he's never going to call me again. His voice is lodged in my head, while the rest of him is running through my veins. He's gone. The man who taught me to stand on my own two feet, to show the world that I fucking matter. He gave me strength, and now I feel so damn weak without him." Her face is blurry, but I see her pain, her agony. More importantly, I see her strength, her confidence in me.

"Let it all out, Roan. Lean on me. Trust me when I tell you that once you let it out, you'll find you're not weak at all. You're strong because of him. You're the man I'm proud to call my husband and the father of our son and our soon-to-be-born child. A weak man wouldn't be sitting here in front of me admitting his feelings. Only a strong and honorable man would, Roan. I promise you, you'll feel so much better if you just let it out. Scream, cry, it doesn't matter; just don't hold it in anymore." I understand why she's blurred in my vision when her hands lift to cradle my face like I am hers. She's wiping away my tears. Tears I didn't even realize I was shedding until now. With my beautiful, pregnant wife on my desk, in the early morning hours, I cry. I let it out, all of it. The loss will always be there. I hope Alina is right that only a strong man admits his fears. Fears and weakness will get me killed.

"You can quit, beautiful lady," I tell her, then I express my sorrow through the tears I finally shed for my dad's death.

I've showered and called my mom to give her the news in hopes it would cheer her up; thankfully, it did in the best way. Like my dad, she worships Alex. Adding this baby to our family will be a blessing in more ways than one. Now, I'm standing in my office again, only this time, I'm listening to Aidan on speakerphone as he defines the details of the small funeral for Bronzer and his beloved wife. It's a shame not one of us can be there to pay our respects to two people whose lives meant nothing to those despicable people who are cowards for coming after me like that. Shame has me staring out the window as I silently promise that once this is all over, they will receive the full-on party to celebrate two wonderful lives that were taken early out of hate so vengeful it's consuming me with guilt.

I'd be lying if I didn't say losing it in Alina's arms didn't help ease some of the pain that has ripped me wide open, left me raw enough that every strike these fuckers cast upon me seers into me like a leech that's embedded far enough into my skin that the only thing that will kill it is to burn its slimy flesh. The anger stage has taken over possessively now in my grieving, and there is nothing like knowing the devil is the one leading the pack to wipe these sons of bitches off our map. To kill them and demolish their entire army. I'm bringing them all down. But first, I have a plan. A plan I need Aidan's help with once again. I need my family securely safe and away from all of this.

"I appreciate you taking care of everything, man. How are you holding up? Were you able to get their ashes?" Cain wanted their ashes brought here. He thought it would be our way of honoring them the next time we all went to Florida by sprinkling them in the ocean where they could always roam free.

"Yeah. His brother let me have them."

"Good, and the money?" I ask.

"All deposited." I close my eyes knowing the city of Detroit accepted my million-dollar donation to be distributed evenly amongst their many homeless shelters in Bronzer and Priscilla's name. They volunteered at several of them over the years. It's a memorial I know would make them happy.

When I open my eyes, they roam the yard. I stare at the guards outside walking the property with guns hidden from my kid's view. It's wrong to feel like a prisoner in your own home. Fucking damn wrong. As much as it pains me, Alina and Alex need to leave here with me. Things are going to get messy. I'm not going to be around to protect them, and I'll be damned if I'm leaving them in the hands of anyone else anymore.

"To answer your other question, I'm good. Deidre and the kids are good. They're safe. And you?" he asks back.

"I'm getting there. Can you stop by tonight? We need to talk about getting everyone out to my mom's house. I'm talking everyone, Aidan."

~

"You ready to go outside, buddy?" I ask Alex, whose smile and squeals light up this entire room. He's racing for the door while I chase him. It's early evening. We've had dinner with my mom and Aunt Cecily, Anna, Deidre, and all the kids who temporarily moved in today. My uncle is on his way here with Cain, Justice, and Calla, who didn't balk at the idea either. She agreed one hundred percent that we should all be together. It's the calm before the storm, the ripple of the waves before the surge. It's all coming; I can feel it in my bones, this fight, battle, and war. Tonight though, family surrounds me. I'm at peace for the first time in a month. I don't know how the hell Aidan pulled off getting everyone together and out he like he did. The only thing that matters is, as soon as the others arrive, we can all be under one roof as a family. Aidan will stay inside the house with the women and children. And Dilan, well, he's working on everything I need to be done with Lorenzo at the moment. I expect him out here with his parents tonight as well. Time stands still, and yet shit gets done when you all come together. I'm thankful Anna's mom and stepfather, Ramsey, along with Deidre's parents, are on some damn safari in the middle of the fucking jungle somewhere. Unharmed and safe.

And hearing my mom finally coming out of her room after I called her to ask if we could all stay with her has me smiling. She didn't ask why. The woman knows everything that's been going on now that she's stopped taking those pills right after I told her about our friend's deaths. I felt she had the right to know, especially with everyone being around her. I would hate for someone to slip up in front of her, for her to feel like I'm hiding things. Of course, she put on a front with her emotions, her eyes giving herself away. She feels the guilt. The rawness of her personal nerves is unraveling, exactly like mine. The only thing she doesn't know yet is the discovery of my brother's involvement. I'll take that information to my grave before I expose her to the possibilities of reliving his loss again.

Alina was more than disappointed when I told her what I felt needed to be done. I know she hates leaving our home. Once I told her it would ease my mind, knowing she's here to help keep an eye on my mom, she caved and agreed. On top of that, a few of her brothers will be on security duty along with her parents coming here daily; Ivan helping guide me and her mom enjoying fussing over Alina and Alex. It will be good for them to all be together. Seeing my mom interact earlier with

Alex made her realize how right I am. She's been as worried about her as I have. And now, here they sit on the back porch, chatting away about Alex and talking to the baby in Alina's stomach, while I scoop my son up in one arm and his soccer ball in the other.

The guards here are nothing new to Alex. In fact, he tries to get them to play when we step out into the warm night. They oblige him for a moment by kicking it and laugh as his short little legs run after it, only to dive on top of it to make it stop.

"He's full of it. Eh?" Liam Septer says with his Canadian slang tacked on the end. As long as I've lived in the Detroit area, then in Canada, I still don't get that shit, but whatever. Liam's been the head of my dad's security for years; now he's mine. A close friend, family, and a reliable confidant stands next to me as we watch Alex try to pick the ball up and toss it like a baseball to Aidan and his son.

"He is. Worth every breath I take to watch him play. He's been driving us nuts wanting to go outside. I appreciate what you've done on such short notice, Liam." I shift my body to shake his hand while keeping an eye on my boy as Liam takes hold of my outstretched hand in a firm and reassuring shake. Liam doubled security at all of our houses, including the drive out here, as well as helped get us out of the house unnoticed.

"I'd do anything for all of you, Roan. Your family is safe here; you can trust me on that. You stay out of that office; you surround yourself with this." We both watch Diesel and Alex's expressions of delight, their purity glowing with their invisible angelic halos.

"What is it you're not telling me?" I sense he's holding back on crucial information. Whether he hasn't the slightest idea how to tell me or he simply wants to give me the time I need with my son. More than likely both, but whatever it is, he knows it's going to rip me apart. Add another bomb we need to disengage before it explodes in our faces.

I keep my mouth shut while I wait for Liam to get whatever is troubling him off his back, allowing our conversation to remain light. I play with my son. I challenge Diesel, who is quick for a toddler his age. We all banter back and forth. My son is trying his hardest to get the eye-foot coordination down. It's comical watching his face morph into a serious expression. His forehead crinkles, and his tongue licks his lips. I stop paying attention when Liam says something that has my back going rigid and the short hairs on the back of my neck shooting straight up.

"You do realize they are an open target now, right?" Both Aidan and I stop playing immediately. Our ears are perking up like a dog's hearing a strange noise. I have no idea where he's going with this, and by the look of concern and confusion on Aidan's face, neither does he. Who is he referring to? Alina? My mom? Calla? All of them?

"She, he, me. We've always been a target." I point one finger toward the house, the other toward Aidan, then one in the center of my chest. I speak the truth to him. He should know this better than anyone, so what the hell is he going on about and why now?

He shakes his head as if he expects me to comprehend what he's trying to say.

"No, Roan. Those women in there are all more vulnerable now. Listen to me carefully," he says low enough for only me to hear. I fling my head in Aidan's direction and wait until he pulls the boys out of earshot.

"What the fuck is going on, Liam?" I say through gritted teeth. Whatever the hell it is, I can smell the rotten vibes radiating off of him that it's another blow to my cracked open chest.

"I have voiced my opinion time and again to your dad about my gut feeling. Don't get me wrong when I say this. He was a smart man with a weakness very few people knew about." It becomes eerily quiet. Even my son's laughter, his childish gibber, has faded.

"What the hell are you talking about, Liam," I say as my body becomes tight, my fist clenching at my sides.

"I'm talking about Hector. His brother. Your dad trusted him. I don't."

CALLA

I roll my neck around in circles trying to ease the tension as we drive out of the city heading toward my aunt's. My dad is behind the wheel of the gray SUV. Cain is sitting on the other side of Justice, who is passed out in between us in her booster seat in the back of the car. After a day of baking cookies and putting together Justice's Lego dollhouse for the tenth time, only to watch her play with it for ten minutes before she moved onto something else, I'm exhausted.

Along with the pain over the loss of our friends, the worry about Cain and his quiet behavior most of the day as he grieves and blames himself is weighing heavily on my heart. He's been trapped in his mind today. The knuckles on his hands are raw from beating on his punching bag. He's tense, distracted, and there's nothing I can do to help him until we're alone. And now, with the phone call I received from Roan, demanding we all move into the Diamond home, I can't help but feel something else isn't right. That another bomb is about to explode in our faces. I hate feeling like with every step I take, I have to weave my body, my feet moving left and right trying to avoid an invisible tripwire. This intense feeling I have now though is the one that settles deep in your bones when you know a storm is coming; your body becomes tight, and your nerves go up in flames. My intuition is feeling this storm brewing. The way the trees murmur when a gust of wind stirs up, the air becomes thick before the sky opens up, and bullet-sized raindrops pelt down on you from the angry skies above.

The word 'angry' describes how I feel. I'm angry at the world. Angry at Cain for placing this on himself. Angry at the man who is behind all of this. Just thinking about this vicious word makes me want to spit nails into Donal, who reminds me of the human form of the evil spirit. He's attacking us as if he's indestructible as he continues to dangle the carrot, just begging for us to take a bite of the poison-infused vegetable that will soon destroy us all.

He reminds me of a weak man, one who hides in the background. A leader who doesn't give a shit about anyone but himself. That's what he's doing. I know it, feel it in the inner depth of my soul that he is sitting back with a smug look on his face, while others go out and cause us the pain that turns into anger so severe it's controlling my every thought. Consuming me in a way no case of one of my accused clients has done before.

I'd give anything, randomly speaking, of course, to interview this egotistical bastard just to see how much of a manipulative psychopath he really is. To look him square in the eye before I cipher that one question of 'why' out of his head. To make him talk. He has us all running around like a chicken with its head cut off, flapping our wings in a frantic motion, and I've had it with him. It's time to face off with this peasant little fucker who dares to try and undermine or ridicule my family into submission. His messages saying he's watching us are done. I don't care what we have to do to get Lorenzo to fight for him. I want it done and over with.

I understand why Roan wants us all together. That's the type of man he is, to protect his own securely before the striking hits. It wasn't his call that angered me; it was his tone. Serious and demanding, as if he too has that same sense of more terror about to strike our family before we have the chance to get him interested in Lorenzo. It's a long shot by far to get him to take an interest in the kid, let alone get him to agree to a fight. The only choice we have is to trust that Lenny knows his son, and that Lorenzo can handle being on the inside. Jesus. The more I think about it, the more scared I am for this young man who has no clue what this kind of life is about. He could wind up dead. Hell, this Irish piece of shit could have someone on the inside from our organization working for him. It happens all the time. Greed or lies make them break their code of silence, turn them into rats.

"Nothing happened, Calla. I give you my word. We will talk when you get here," Roan had said. Talk about what? I thought we were moving forward, that they had a plan in motion, and now this.

"You doing okay back there, Calla?" My heart skips a beat, stutters before it kicks into a quick beating rhythm in my chest when I catch a hint of the one emotion I've felt or heard radiating off of my dad: fear. My eyes dart over to Cain, who has his closed, his arm securely around our daughter. He's either deep in thought or giving me time to talk to my dad. With the way guilt ate away at him like he was its favorite food today, I would say both. He hated not being able to be there for his longtime friends. To say goodbye to two people who meant the world to him.

"I will be," I tell him.

"What's running through your mind, sweetheart? Talk to me," he barrels out like the worried father he is.

I stare out the window before I respond, not knowing where to start. My adventurous mind is spiraling out of control with questions and the right words to answer that will lead to more as I untangle them all in my problematic head.

"A little nervous about having her out in the open," I speak loud enough for him to hear, yet soft enough not to wake her. I won't feel safe until I have her tucked firmly into bed tonight. Truthfully, I doubt I'll feel that safety until this is resolved. I may never feel that emotion again. Hell, if I dig deeper into the truth, I haven't felt it in years. I've only shoved it to the back of my mind. The uncertainty of never feeling it again has weighed heavily on my chest since the day we lost my uncle. My gaze immediately drifts down to her sleeping form; her head is tilted toward her dad. Her protector. Her idol. I shiver at the thought of anything happening to this innocent child. Or anyone else in my circle at all. I'm scared, and the only person I will admit it to is my very own hero, who I can feel staring back at me through the review mirror in this dark and gloomy box I'm trapped in.

"I feel the same way about you being out. Her too. All of you, Calla. I worry about every single one of you. This is some serious shit, how this tool has snuck up on us out of nowhere, striking us in the center of our heart before branching out to hit every nerve. I'm going to tell you something; you need to let it seep in, let it absorb you. It needs to take over your life. Nothing else can exist right now. Do you understand me?" His voice is stern with an edginess I rarely hear from him. It's crisp and pristine. Laced with knowledge, determination, and fright.

"I understand." I manage to pull out strength from God knows where. I can't have him worrying when he's about to enter the world he's lived in for decades all over again. To kill. I worry about him too. He used to be the best. Even though he hasn't killed anyone in years, well, not to my knowledge anyway, he's still the best in my eyes. The thing is, he's getting older. He isn't as quick as he was. My dad tries to hide the aches and pains that have taken over his body the older he gets. I see them though, the changes. The way his gait is still strong, yet slower. The way his hands shake slightly sometimes.

"I'll be fine, Calla," he says as if he can read my mind. "Your old man may be older, but never doubt that I will kill someone before they have the chance to know I'm even there. I may be rusty, but I have one thing these assholes don't have. I have love. I have an entire family I'm not ready to give up yet." I'm sure his words are meant to reassure me; they don't. My uncle was full of love and protection, and to be blunt, he was killed while exiting a restaurant. A man, whose guard was never down, just like my dad. The unexpected can happen at any time; this is what scares me the most.

"I'm your daughter, old man. Like you, I'll worry. Now, quit reading my thoughts and tell me what you think I need to know." We've already had the discussion of me reining in my fear, never to let them see me weak or falter, and for me to make certain taking on this new role was something I wanted as well as could handle. So whatever it is he needs for me to hear and understand has peaked my curiosity to the point I'm despearte to hear it. He's a wise man, has the knowledge like no other. When a man like John Greer speaks, you listen.

"You need to do everything, and I mean everything, Roan tells you, Calla. Do not argue with him. Do not question his motives or his reasons. You may feel like he's not telling you everything, and he more than likely won't, not right now anyway. For his sake as well as yours, do what he says. He's been thrown into a role he's not entirely prepared for, just like you. He needs to know you support him, without the questions of why to follow. Do this one thing this one time for me, sweetheart?" A part of me wants to lash out at my dad and ask him why he's asking this of me. I'm not a defiant person. Stubborn and pessimistic maybe, but Jesus, when it comes to my family, I'm as protective as the rest of them. More so now with Roan. Especially with how overloaded his plate is. Roan's strings are being pulled tight in every direction. Loss, love, family, and worry. Those things alone can cause a person's strings to snap and unravel in a dangerous way. I bite my tongue instead of asking him why. Deep down I know it's all for my own good as well as everyone else's. I don't hesitate at all to consider what he's saying. Dad is telling me that if Roan makes one mistake, it could wind up destroying us all. He needs to remain focused right now on bringing these people down, on destroying them before they can do any more damage to him, before he loses control and flies off the handle in a rage of revenge without thinking it through completely. Therefore, I'm to remain silent. Keep the guns coming in and the trades going out. I'm going to keep our empire running.

"Of course, I..." That's all I manage to get out before Cain is jerking up into a sitting position. His hand is lashing out across Justice, who is immediately startled awake as the vehicle swerves off the road to avoid a car that veered into our lane so fast it caused my dad to lose control of the wheel. Dad outrights the SUV back onto the road, the back end rebounding, tires squealing as he steers it back into position and pressing on the gas in a sudden maneuver that has me gripping the headrest on his seat with shaky hands. It's dark out this way, with only the streetlights and the soft glow of the moon radiating down on the ocean. I've traveled this road many times. I know it by heart. We're only a few miles from the Diamond Estate; he needs to slow down before he winds up having an accident.

"Calla, get down." My dad's calm voice drifts from the front before I have the chance to tell him he's scaring me. Something is wrong. Flashbacks from our accident years ago hit me. The sound of crunching metal, undistinguished noises that grate your ears until they feel like exploding, have me in a panic as I lean over and put my arms around my daughter. I'm shaking as the fear crawls up my neck. God, the last time nearly cost both Roan and me our lives. It cost Cain and me to lose our baby. What if they run us off the road and take her, or worse yet, something happens to her? I remain calm for her sake alone as I listen to Cain bolter out to someone on the phone to get their asses out here.

"Whoever it is has turned around and is gaining speed." Cain looks back. Our eyes meet when he shifts forward. He's as worried as I am. He glances from me to her, then back to her again, where he lingers for a moment before he reaches my eyes once again with a look of fright. I exhale, then look down to the silvering gleam in his hand. He's already holding his gun in his lap, hidden from Justice's view.

I want to scream as badly as he wants to spin around and pull that trigger on whoever the hell is trying to scare us. Both of us know he can't because of the life sitting next to us. The life that is more precious than the three of ours combined. My dad remains calm while my insides shake with fear like I've never known before. My throat dries. I feel like I'm being choked from the inside. I can't breathe. My God, what if they hit us from behind or shoot as us? It would scare her, or worse yet, we could crash. They could take her like I was taken. I want to scream and yell for them to stop. My heart beats wildly in my chest, each thump louder, angrier, and frantically ringing in my ears. I want them dead for bringing this fear into my world. A fear so deep I can feel it bouncing from my dad to Cain to me, spinning like the vicious cycle the persecutor behind us wants. Whoever is doing this, knows. They fucking know she's in here with us. There isn't anyone who saw us leave; the only ones who know are those we trust. It all hits me at once, this fear of the unknown helplessness that slinks up my spine and embarks on the center of my heart. Fear that turns my anger so fierce I could kill someone. Fear that summons my muddled thoughts into the desire to grab Cain's gun and shoot them myself.

"Daddy. What's happening?" Justice asks in her soft, sleepy voice. Her little head is pressed against my shoulder, my hands trying to cover her ears in case he belts out something he shouldn't. My instincts as a mother are kicking in to protect her without her knowing it. She's too young to understand any of this. I see my husband fighting within himself to say something to keep her calm. Demons, we all have them. Right now, I'm not sure if God is trying to test us or if the devil himself is doing everything he can to bring us down. Either way, this situation involving my child is a cruel punishment.

"Papa wants to hurry and get you to see Nana," he answers shakily. I close my eyes, stroking her hair as the sweat trickles down my back.

Cain's emotions have to be clawing at him from the inside out. The not being able to talk or tell my dad to bring the vehicle to a stop so he can blow their heads off is killing him. I have never wished death on a person as much as I do now. The smell of it absorbs me to the brink of insanity. This is our world right here between us, and they have just dug their own grave.

His phone rings before she asks anything more. Her tiny body is trembling in my shaky arms. He looks down at it, then back to me. It's easy to read his expression with the car behind us close enough that the headlights are hitting the back of our seats. He has no idea who it is. My guess, it's them letting us know they are sending us a warning of some kind. *Well, no fucking shit, you bastards. I'm holding your warning in my arms.* He leans forward and answers with a clipped and muffled hello.

"That will never happen," he says sternly. "My daughter is in this vehicle. Think twice before you do anything." With those words, his phone falls to the floor, while his head stays pressed to the front seat. How the hell did they get his phone number?

It seems like forever as my dad speeds down the road in this stuffy, tension-filled vehicle when in actuality, it's only a minute or so until Cain's phone rings again. He picks it up. I hear Aidan's booming voice telling us he believes he sees our headlights. Cain mumbles something into the phone I can't hear then hangs up once again, only this time, he sits up and shoves the phone into his back pocket, while the gun hidden from Justice's view slides into the waistband of his jeans. I stay crouched over my girl, who, thank God, is oblivious once again as I mumble how much I love her and just want to cuddle with her until we get there. She seems appeased with this; she loves to cuddle herself. It's not until we pull up to the gate, which is wide open, that my husband opens the door and jumps out, startling both Justice and me. It slams shut. Her head snaps up, her arms reaching for her dad. He's gone. The car following us whizzes by, followed by screeching tires, which I know has to be Aidan chasing after them with Cain in the car with him. My God, it all happens so fast, I've lost my breath. I lift my head, my arm still around my daughter, my eyes looking at the bright, lit-up mansion in front of us. Then, and only then, do I feel myself breathe.

"Why did Daddy jump out? It's dark out there, Mommy," Justice asks with a puzzled look on her face the minute we stop in front of the house.

"Did you hear your daddy on the phone?" my white knight savior of a father says.

"I heard it ring," she says curiously.

"That was Uncle Aidan on the phone. They had to go get something for Nana," my dad answers.

"Nana. I want to see her. She promised to read my new book to me. Did you bring it, Mommy?" Her sweet voice should calm me down, the way she's unmindful of the events surrounding her. My dad's mention of my mother is enough to make her forget about her question altogether. My hands are shaking uncontrollably as I fumble with the buckle on her seat. All I want to do is get her in the house and away from all the guards I see rushing toward the vehicle. I know what's about to happen here. Whoever is in that vehicle will be caught and brought here. They will be taken to the barn, the place I've never been in since my uncle had it built a little over a year ago. It's a hidden underground basement of some kind that rests below his multi-car unattached garage. A place where he stored his prized collection of old cars and motorcycles. No one would ever suspect he has that torture chamber down there. It's been forbidden by Cain for me to go there. He says shit happens down there I wouldn't be able to handle. Well, not anymore. Tonight, they overstepped their boundaries. They are dealing with an uncontrollable mother who will cut their goddamn balls off and stuff them down their throats for the stunt they pulled tonight.

I have no doubt in my mind they will capture whoever that is and bring them back here for a thorough interrogation before they kill them.

My anger boils over the more I think about the barn and the closer I get to the inside of the house with my daughter pressed close and my dad's hand on my back.

I'm going in there with them, whether they like it or not.

ROAN

"What the hell do you mean, you don't trust Hector? That is a hell of a lot of baggage to be tossing at me when I'm dealing with some psychopathic organization that could cause the entire state to erupt if we don't get a handle on this in a goddamn hurry, Liam." I'm damn near foaming at the mouth. I'm bleeding out from one thing to the next. My head is in a constant state of instability here, in the eye of a storm, where it doesn't matter which direction I take, the wind picks up violently and spins me into its counter-clockwise tunnel as the storm front picks up speed and sadistically tries to dissolve my fucking sanity. How in the fuck did my dad know who to trust? I trust Hector, and I trust Liam, and now I feel as if Liam unintentionally has a knife to my back, pleading with me to hear him out before Hector sneaks up and stabs me with a knife of his own. Fuck.

Hector is blood; my dad may not have claimed him publicly, but we all know the reason why. It was for his protection. He works with the cops, for Christ's sake. Other associations would shit him out in pieces after they slaughtered him if they were to find out who he is. My dad trusted him. He also trusted Liam. So what in the ever-loving hell is going on here?

"Keep an eye on Alex for a few." I turn around with my back facing the two of them, my front to Liam, after Aidan lifts his chin, letting me know he will watch Alex while I talk.

"You and your father have always had huge hearts. You give more than you take. You listen, you care about your family and friends, and you protect with all you have. Now, with that being said, what I'm about to say you can do with what you want, but I'm warning you as I warned him, don't shove it aside, Roan. I'm going to be blunt. I took a chance with telling your dad, but he wouldn't listen, and now he's gone. He never listened when it came to Hector. He told me to shut the hell up, to never bring it up again. So I didn't. But you bet I kept my eyes and ears open. That man is toxic, Roan. I can smell the poison leaking out of him. He is jealous of the man your dad was. He wants the Diamond Empire. Don't ask me how I know this, I just do. He's playing you all. He has been for years. I wouldn't be shocked if he wasn't in on this with Royal, if he was the traitor feeding inside information to the Irish." If what he's saying is true, then Hector is as fucked up as this Irish cocksucker. He will never make it. His status of being a private investigator will send up red flags for the men he works with to the goddamn President. He'll be dead before he takes charge. I close my eyes, thinking of my brother once again. Liam had to go and tack on the one name that we all know had something to do with my dad's death, didn't he? I see red, nothing but pent-up anger, blood fucking red. Hearing my brother's name zaps a surge of rage through me. He's dead, and yet he's like a goddamn rare poker hand. A Royal fucking flush that is rarely dealt. A rarity that is hard to wrap your head around, because no matter how many poker hands you are dealt, the probability of getting a Royal Flush is next to nothing. But the prospect of a man named Royal Diamond to surprise you with his winning hand from death is beating every goddamn odd out there.

"This wavering of his loyalty of yours is all based off of a hunch," I vilely say through clenched teeth and hands that are balled into fists. Not at this man who would never steer me wrong; it's because now he has those crucial ifs and buts raging through my mind. "Jesus Christ, Liam. I know you would never speak of distrust if you didn't believe it. But fuck, man, I can't just snatch him up and beat him down, demanding to know if he had anything to do with my dad's death without proof. He's a crooked man. You know as well as I do the things he has done for us. He's killed people. Ratted some of the dirty idiots who ratted on us when they got pinched. Stole evidence. Fuck, he's done it all. Dirty or not, every one of those cops he works with would be up my ass. Unless... Jesus, Liam." It hits me like a startling crack of thunder followed by a blinding white sheet of lightning striking my brain. I tumble backward a step, my brain on fire with that deep crimson color. My throat is drying up just like that. My imagination is running wild while I stare blankly past Liam into the glistening water from the swimming pool. Jesus Christ, it's true.

"He's been promised protection from the Irish if he helps them ruin us, if he kills as many of us as he can." My voice is strained from saying those words that stab my heart like a dagger. Every ounce of my body feels like deflating when I think of the many meals, gifts, and money, and, most importantly, the unconditional love my dad and our family extended to Hector and his. Dad felt guilty from the first day he found out they were brothers. I was too young to remember how he found out about my grandfather's infidelity, but I remember the joyous expression on his face whenever he talked about the sibling he'd found. I feel fucking sick. First, *my* brother betrays us, and now my dad's. What in the fuck is wrong with people? My dad would have welcomed that man into this organization without a care what anyone thought at all, because he loved him. He would have given him the protection he needed.

Waged his own reputation that Hector was loyal to our organization and not trying to bring us down. Is greed to these sick fuckers worth the lives of others? Obviously, it is. It isn't to me. What is important to me is revenge. And if this is true, then Hector will never see me coming.

"Get me the proof I need," I rattle, then turn to spend only five fucking minutes longer with my son before Aidan answers his phone and all hell breaks loose again.

"Get him in the house now." Aidan startles the hell out of Liam and me when he hangs up his phone. The look in eyes is like none other. He's frightened.

Without saying anything, I pick up my son and make my way into the house, where Alina is waiting at the door. She looks up to see me with a horrified expression on my face.

"What's happening?" she asks, her voice panicked and strained.

"Just take him and go upstairs," Aidan demands. I stop in my tracks, my eyes pleading for her to do as he asks. I'm waiting to see what the fuck is going on when Aidan shoves me forward out of my family's earshot. Liam is standing by our side. My mom is hot on our heels, sprouting off for us to tell her what the hell is going on.

"That was Cain on the phone. Someone is trying to run them off the road. They are a few miles from here. Let's move." And just like that, my world stops. The flashbacks, screaming, the waking up to my brother abusing, beating, and pumping Calla full of drugs while he has me tied up, watching him try and break her while he's torturing the fuck out of me. Cutting off my finger. All of it hits me until the flames from years ago ignite in my veins. The urge to kill someone coats my lungs with anticipation to drain the motherfuckers who dare try and hurt my family.

"They have Justice with them. You find them, Roan, and you kill them. You make them pay. Do you hear me?" my Mom rages. Her body shakes from the fury that's shooting out of her. As sickening as it may seem to hear her tell me to kill someone, a sense of happiness swells in my chest seeing hatred radiating off of her instead of sadness.

"They'll pay. Now, let's go," I promise her. It's one thing I'm damn sure of. Aidan and I are out the door without a goodbye or a kiss to my wife. I never leave without kissing her and my son. There's no time for it, not with our family members in danger. I have no damn idea what the hell is going on. All I do know is, before I kill whoever is behind the wheel of that vehicle, they are going to tell me who sent them and why.

It only takes a few moments until we're in Aidan's car and are heading out the gate as we see their SUV approach. "How are Calla and Justice?" I ask Cain when he jumps in the car. We barely stopped to pick him up. All I saw was a glimpse of Calla holding Justice before we sped off down the road after these assholes.

"She's scared out of her mind. Whoever is behind this is going to die a slow death," Cain shouts. His voice is shaky.

"Let me handle this." I proceed to explain what Liam told me about his suspicions of Hector as we quickly approach the back of the car that better hold someone to give me answers.

"Jesus motherfucking Christ. I am sick and tired of people who seem to think they can live on both sides of the tracks. Don't they get that there's shit on both sides of the goddamn grass? This would crush your dad." Aidan tells me something I already know. My dad would be devastated if he knew there's a possibility of what Liam claims to hold an ounce of truth. Especially if something would have happened.

I don't go into the details of my knowledge of this, because the vehicle in front of us swerves into a parking lot entrance to one of the many public beaches.

"Stupid fuck." Cain pulls out his gun and barks out a slew of profanities when he rolls down his window and rallies off several shots that hit one of the tires, causing this crazy maniac to try and control the veering, swerving directions his car wants to take. It's no use. He weaves and strays, making it easier on us when he runs head-on into a pole, causing the car to come to a complete stop. Two men scramble out, the passenger disappearing on his side of the car, the driver wobbling on his feet before he comes to his senses and dashes to the other side and out of our sight.

"Give it up, motherfuckers!" I yell when we stop. They start firing their guns at us. I climb over the seat in a hurry, exiting the driver's side behind Aidan, where we shield ourselves with protection from the open door. The gunfire is hitting the car in a sharp sound of bullets hitting metal.

"Fuck you," one of them snarls. The voice is unfamiliar, for now. He's about to become very familiar with my voice, and I with his. He will talk. They both will before we put a bullet right between their goddamn eyes. After I beat them half to death first.

"Man, you have nowhere to go but hell from here. You may as well come out from behind that car. Tell us what we want to know or die a painful death from being burnt alive." I train my gaze on Aidan, who reaches around me with his long body and digs into the glove box, pulls out a flashlight, and shines it right below the fuel door. I know all too well he's not going to blow that fucker up unless he wants the three of us to go up in flames with them. We're met with silence until Aidan fires off shots that blow out both windows on this side of the car. The sound of the shattering glass is echoing throughout the dark, deadly night.

"Damn, brother, you aren't fucking around," Cain says, then moves from his crouching position with me behind him heading straight for the car, while Aidan keeps firing, the clang of the bullets hitting the metal side of the door. If I didn't have the urge to kill, I would laugh at the way this shit looks and feels. It's impossible to ignore the resemblance to a goddamn movie with the stupid fucks on the other side of the car thinking they have it made, and then bam out of nowhere, they have guns pointing in their faces. That's exactly what happens next; only our guns do not have blanks and the blood these two are about to shed will be real. In fact, I might string them up and watch it all drain from the tips of their toes to the tops of their heads and let it channel out from their mouths. I hate these fuckers with a passion so fierce, if I didn't want to know who sent them, I would skin them alive.

"Hello, fuckers," Cain says with a smile on his face when we both point our guns down at the two men. One of them tries to lift his gun. I kick him in the face, knocking him back into the man behind him. Both of them fall to the ground. I quickly grab both of their guns, patting them down to make sure they have no other weapons. Once I'm satisfied they don't, I yank one up by the hair on his head, while Cain grabs the other by the collar of his shirt. We drag them both across the pavement. Their loud condemnations of how we will pay and die cover up the brutal scraping of their flesh being dragged across the pavement. Amateurs.

"The only ones dying tonight are you stupid fucks. Now, get the fuck in." I yank this piece of shit to his feet and look him in the eye. I've never seen him before. Dark hair, dark eyes are staring back at me. A smug look on his face. He's a dead man.

"Suicide mission accomplished, motherfucker," I say with all the revenge I have within me.

"You think this is over," he says sarcastically.

"It's over for you. Now, get the fuck in." I shove him toward Aidan, who tosses him and the other man who looks scared out of his mind into the back of the SUV. Cain jumps in behind them, and before Aidan closes the door, I hear the sound of a fist hitting flesh and groans being made. Threats from Cain. My hands itch as my mind goes into torture mode. I grit my teeth all the way back to the house, welcoming the pain to my jaw. I'm beyond the realms of anger, so far down in the abyss that the need to destroy is all I can see. If I were an animal, I would be foaming at the mouth to rip the heads off of these two. You do not fuck with me or those I love and live to tell the story. I'm a man they should never have screwed with, a man different from the one years ago when I made my first kill to save Anna's life. I vowed then there would be no second chances if you were disloyal to the families' code, dishonor them in the most callous way. You do not come into someone's city and dare start a war. That's all kinds of fucked up. It's modern-day suicide.

All of this is for the revenge I need to honor my dad. To finally rid my family of the demons my brother somehow convinced to destroy us. He may have taken away my hero with his broods of followers who won't live much longer, but I'll die first before I let him rise from the grave like he's some god and hurt anyone else I care about. No, these men will be sent back with a message carved into their bodies for the untamed who dared to think he could cross me by coming after my family.

We make it home in minutes. The moment we come to a stop in front of the barn, Aidan cuts the engine. We both climb out, walk to the back, and help Cain lead these two into the final minutes of their lives. They will die like many others have before them in this place. Beg for it even.

"You two strap him up. Dilan and I have this one." I was stunned but not surprised to see Dilan waiting in the barn for us when we got here. Liam or Uncle John must have told him what was going on. No one else knew that once we captured who we were after, we would bring them back here. Everyone knows about this place, but no one walks through the door who isn't invited. Some brutal, fucked-up shit happens in here. Shit that makes my stomach churn and has bile rising to my throat. Right now though, with my head hammering and the thought of what could have happened if they had caused an accident, I want to drain their blood until nothing is left but rotten corpses.

Usually, we bring in one of our assassins to do the job of torturing and then killing. I had no time to call anyone, but as I watch my uncle stand here with his hands balled at his sides, his eyes dark and out of focus, I'm thankful he's here. I'm glad it's all of us who are going to take a shot at these pussies.

"It's your call on how you want to make them unrecognizable to, what was his name again?" I look at my uncle while I ask anyone in the room who cares to answer. My deep voice is showcasing the hunger I have to get these men to talk. Their eyes are bugging out of their heads, their necks straining as they squirm, shouting all kinds of profanities that are going in one ear and out the other.

"Donal Sweeny." Neither one of them flinches at the name my uncle thunders out, which leads me to believe they weren't sent by the Irish. As much as it pains me to say what I say next, I do it without the sincerity of hurt in my tone or my heart that tells me it's true.

"No, that isn't it. It's Hector Moran," I say while inspecting the face of the one I know isn't going to talk. The other one will squeal like a pig if he thinks there's a chance we won't kill him. I watch for the one little sign that I pray to God I don't see from this dirty fucker. He gives it away with just the slightest jerk to the corner of the mouth. My heart slams into my chest with the knowledge that Hector betrayed us. He is working for the goddamn Irish mob, and these two are working for him.

"Gather some men together and find Hector. He'll know something is up when these fuckers don't return," I convey to Aidan. Then blinding rage takes over as I make my way to the man I'm going to kill. "And Aidan," I say as I stare this soon-to-be ghost of a man down with a look that should knock him dead right here. "Strap him down in the electric chair. Then ask Liam to help you keep him company until we get there." I watch my target's eyes go wide, then I wait for Aidan to leave before I speak in a low, deadly voice.

"That's what happens to dirty cops, investigators, or pieces of trash like you who try and fuck us over. We burn their flesh. So tell me, which one are you? A cop perhaps?" He smirks. His stare meant to intimidate me only fuels my desire to tear the skin off his pretty-boy face.

"He's not a cop. He's a bleat. A lamb they toss out to be slaughtered. Both of them are," Uncle John speaks then places a knife directly under the other guy's chin. I'm not sure why I know the other one will talk while this crazy asshole will take the beating of a lifetime before he will snitch. It might be the fact that when I turn my head to give my uncle the orders he's craving to hear, he's standing there pissing himself as I watch the front of his light-colored jeans darken from his urine.

"Make him talk then cut out his tongue and shove it down his throat." A strangled cry comes from the man when I see my uncle slice the knife across the bottom of his chin, causing blood to trickle down his corded, veined neck.

"You're going to tell me why you tried to get my daughter. It's her your pussy motherfucking boss wants, isn't it?" he demands from the guy, who simply nods.

"Answer him." Cain approaches and points a gun at his temple.

"Yes," is his reply.

A maddening hiss comes from the guy in front of me, and I jerk my head in his direction. He struggles against the ropes to get himself free. The one wrapped around his neck turns his skin red and raw. Blood begins to dribble out from underneath the rope. That has to burn like a bitch. Both of them are tied to wooden beams in the middle of the room. He has nowhere to go, but like the dumbass he is, he fights against that thick rope to free himself. He needs to learn a lesson. My fist connects with his jaw, then another with his stomach. He groans; I grunt. Every time his head drops, Dilan is there to lift it back up so I can deliver more. I continue to beat the living shit out of the guy who says nothing to my questions about Hector or Donal, while the other one screams, pleads, and begs for his life. I nearly pummel this fucker to death. My hands burn with every punch I throw. The blood from his face splatters onto my face and clothes, and still I don't stop, not until I've taken the pent-up anger searing through me out on him. In between me tearing the flesh off this man's face, I hear the other guy telling them they work for Hector, who works for the Irish. He has no clue if it's Donal or not. He was only told to get Calla and bring her to Hector. My blood boils, my vision blurs at his words.

"I'm done here." My vision begins to fade from red to black. I want out of here. I'm wasting my time with this crazy, brainwashed asshole who now has my soul raging in flames. My voice is raspy from yelling at this man who refuses to talk. We now know who is behind this. Once Aidan finds him, he too will pay for the sins he has cast against us. For the death of my dad. For it all. I take a step back, pull out my gun, and the minute Dilan is out of the way, I shoot him right between his eyes.

CALLA

Quietly, I sneak out of the bedroom Justice is sleeping in. Once she was snuggled up to my mom, who was reading her a book, her tiny little eyelids struggled to remain open. I glance at my beautiful little girl so full of life and thank God we were close to this house before anything could have happened to her. Then I look to my mom, who briefly lifts her head and gives me the same tender gaze I've been giving my child. If it weren't for her and my aunt, I would more than likely be on my way to the barn right now. They talked me out of it.

The minute my dad left to head there, I told her what I wanted to do. Her response made sense. "Your dad would not want you to see what goes on in there, Calla." I gauged my mood listening to her tell me that in spite of my need to seek revenge, it was not my job. It's theirs, and no matter how I feel, the things that go on in there would haunt me for life.

"They aren't the men we know when they enter that place, sweet girl.

Trust me on this. You would not want to witness any of it." A cold shiver ran down my spine when she spoke. My thoughts ran wild with images of blood and broken bones. Men screaming ran through my head. Pictures of my husband taking another's life. It all became too much to bear.

Even though I know she was right, it still doesn't calm me down. The only thing that will is seeing the men I love walk through the door. Safely.

I silently walk down the hall to the bedroom Cain and I will share, hesitating outside my aunt's door. It's closed, yet light trickles out from underneath, indicating she is up waiting for me. She was furious when we'd walked in, her eyes narrow and rigid until she took Justice out of my arms; then they softened like melted butter, pooled with unshed tears.

If I hadn't heard the words fall from her lips a while later, I would have been shocked she stayed put in this house instead of following the guys. I place my hand over my heart as I stand in the dimly lit hallway, her words from earlier heating up my soul, making me learn a hard lesson in this life I thought I'd already been accustomed to.

"You may stand by my son's side, Calla Lily, but don't ever think the power you have is yours to do with as you wish. Not when it comes to drawing blood from another. A lot of things have changed in the way our world works; one that will never change, at least not in this family, is we prevent our women from having blood on their hands unless they are given no choice. You let them handle it." I wanted to push everything both her and my mom said to me aside. Their words mixing with those of my dad's created my sanity to reappear. Even though I wanted to tell them I'm stronger than they think, that I could handle it, the truth is they are right. I'm not a killer. Not unless I have no choice.

She grinned next, tucked my hair behind my ear, and then held my face in her hands. Her eyes shined bright with pride. She knew her words were sinking in about my place in our family not being that of a killer. I was born to help lead this family's business. To investigate, put my lawyer skills to work. To be behind the scenes and surface when I needed to.

"You remind me of your mother in every way, sweet girl. So strong, so independent. You have such thick skin. A woman who only knows how to vilify and pull someone to pieces in the courtroom is now one of my family's leaders. You lead where Roan tells you, you advise him where he needs it. Listen and learn to those who know what it's like to live with taking a life of another. Like your dad, Roan, and Cain. That barn is not a place for you, nor me. Don't become someone you are not. You are a leader, not a killer." This time, tears fell down her aged face. I reached up and swiped them away. "I hate this for us. For you." My voice broke, and my mind gave in to the anger and fear that were pent up inside. I cried with her. She held me close after that. Her sadness and loss are a weight on her tiny shoulders. She has lost so much. A son, her husband, and still she stood tall. I should have been the one to hold her, to try and make her feel better, help heal her broken heart. Instead, she took care of me. She made me understand the path that's laid out before me. The role I play in this family. I'm to stand alongside these men, lead when I am needed, be strong for my husband when he returns. Killing another isn't easy for anyone, no matter who you are.

Even though we said goodnight earlier, I whisper it once again through the wooden door before I carry my tired body down the hall. I make my way across the plush carpet through the dark and into the bathroom, where I flip on the light switch over the mirror that brightens the room enough to set off a relaxing, spa-like glow. Stripping my clothes off, I step into the large, luxurious walk-in shower and push the button for the main showerhead that begins to rain down the heavy water I need to cleanse away this fear. Once I have the water set to my liking, I step under the spray, resting my hands in front of me while letting the water beat down on top of my aching head. The entire evening is replaying in my mind.

I jump when I feel familiar hands wrap around my waist, pulling me into his hard, expansive chest.

"How is she?" I turn in Cain's arms until our gazes meet. The only things I see are his worry and concern for our little girl. There is no guilt, no remorse for what went on, for what I know they did. I know better than to ask him about it. The need to know if he's okay with what he's done, with what he's been doing for years now, is still there waiting to slip off the end of my tongue. I swallow it, grab his scruffy face in my hands, and put him out of his misery.

"She's the same sweet little girl she's been since the day she was born," I express happily.

"You sure?" God, this man standing gloriously naked in front of me is who my mom wants me to remember. The tough exterior, the soft interior. I see it now with the way he rubs his hands up and down my back. The way he runs his fingers through my long, wet hair. This is my Cain. The man who loves with all he has. Our protector.

"Did she not look okay when you checked on her?" I lift a brow. A cocky smirk curls upward on my lips. I know damn well he looked in on her before he came in here.

"She did." He nuzzles my neck, his wet lips connecting with my sweet spot that turns me inside out.

"Tell me you're okay too, because right now, I need to be inside of you." I respond to his question with an astute moan, then a sharp bite on his nipple that sends him into the savage lover he is. I need him to make it all go away. The maddening heartache, these sheltering walls. My idiotic thoughts of wanting to kill. All of it.

His hands float down to grip my ass, and he smashes his lips to mine in a beastly kiss. He kisses me like he knows my thoughts. As if he hasn't seen me for days. It's rough, grueling even, the way he sucks my tongue into his mouth, his lips fusing to mine like a sheer coated lip balm penetrating its cure with one solid swipe. He leaves me breathless.

The minute his mouth leaves mine, my hands fist his hair; his mouth scales down my jaw and latches onto my neck, sending a hot, electric force starting from the spot his mouth sucks and licks to the tips of my toes. Pulses start to thump between my legs. I ache for him. I need him to make love to me.

"I need you to love me, Cain," I tell him with a punch of intensity from deep within my throat.

"Turn around. Place your hands on the tile and let me see that sweet ass." I look down at his thick, heavy cock, his veins protruding through the colorful skin. I spin around, palms to the tile, the water running down my back, and I bend slightly, my ass right there for his viewing pleasure.

"Goddamn, if I didn't need to be inside of your sweet cunt, I would fuck this ass." He slaps both cheeks at the same time. My body is jolting forward, pleasure rippling through me.

"You can have my ass later." His expression is priceless when I turn my head and peer over my shoulder at him. It's the look of the devil himself, a carnal man on a mission to capture his prized possession.

"Oh, baby. I'll take your pussy slow, fast, and hard right now, make sweet love to you whenever you want me to. But this ass, I'll take it any goddamn time you let me. Get ready to scream, Calla. I'm about to leave you breathless." His dirty talk, his deep, blazing, penetrating eyes as they bore into mine with love, desire, and the need for me have every muscle except one relaxing, the one between my legs; it jumps in anticipation for what's to come. Aches to the point of pain for him to take me sweetly. My man clearly likes to be in control. Likes to fuck hard and often. Tonight, I need to challenge him any way I can so he will take the pain away. So we both cope with the events of the evening in the way we know best: by connecting, by recreating the dangerous spark that seems to flare up the minute he puts his hands on my body.

"Show me what you got, Mr. Bexley." He grips my hips roughly, thrusting his hardness up against my ass.

"I love you so fucking much," he says while watching himself tease and taunt his dick over my clit, my folds, and my ass.

"I love you too," I say breathlessly. I'm lost in him. There isn't a thing about him I don't love. The way he takes care of us, puts us first, loves us in ways I never deemed possible.

When familiar features cross his face, flaring pupils and parting lips, I know it's time to brace myself, to turn my head back around, close my eyes, and let him take my body the way he loves.

Instinctively, my body stimulates with more arousal when his hand slides across my wet skin and trails down to cup my pussy, spreading my folds to tease my clit with fast, torturous circles. Around and around his finger goes. My chest rises and falls. My breathing becomes rapidly expressive and my pulse thumps in my ears. Every part of me succumbs to his touch as he baits my body into submission.

"Fuck, Calla, I can't hold back." His words are more like a command. I spread my legs and tilt my ass higher, sliding it over his cock. He hisses loudly, then yanks my body back and away from the spray of the water. I crane my neck around just as his back hits the tiled wall for support, my hands bracing on my knees. In one solid, hard thrust, he fills me with the part of his body I need so desperately as our bodies are merging in a heated rush.

"Fuck, babe. Every time I get inside of you, I swear to God I never want to come out." It is all push in slowly and pull out slower after that. His cock is filling me in ways only he knows how, my legs barely holding myself up, my head facing forward. In all the years we've been married, he has never taken me with such desperation as I now feel with every long, deep plunge. I know without a doubt it has everything to do with the fear he felt tonight. He needs this. It's the one thing he knows he has control of as our world shatters around us.

Emotions begin to mix in with the heavy steam, trapping us in an urgency that has me begging him with a silent plea to make me come. To erase it all. I feel how scared we are mixed with our sweat, feel his desperation with every thrust, his fingers filled with fear, our minds filled with a mournful conglomerate of what could have happened tonight. It scares me to the point that yes, our lives could have been taken tonight, our worlds tumbling out of control, that there would be nothing left that would make either one of us recover.

"It's going to be all right, baby. She's safe," Cain tells me as if he can read my thoughts, feel those sensations like I do. I gasp instead of commenting, my thoughts quickly turning to how well we know each other, how good he makes me feel. "I can't see your face, Calla, but I know your plump lips are parted, your eyes are closed, and you need to come. Touch yourself. Let me feel you. Let me take it all away," he says in a low, raspy voice.

"God, Cain." I don't know if I'm pleading or begging for the need to come. I do what he says, while my mind is filled with as much desperation as I hear in his voice.

I shift an unsteady hand to my clit. I rub. I push. I pull. I feel his glistening cock as he slides in and out of me in firm, hard strokes. My eyes are closed like he said; my lips are parted. They always are when I'm close. I see his face, feel his lips whenever I let go. It's always him.

I release my other hand from my knee to cover my scream as he grips my hips and powers into me harder, driving me to the edge. I come hard, lose control while visualizing the lines of concentration on Cain's forehead. His dark eyes are full of love for me. His jaw is slack, his muscles are flexing. Then I feel it. His cock is swelling, his body stilling as he comes inside of me with a faint growl, repeating the words 'I love you' over and over until his body gives out to where he pulls out of me, twirls me around, and kisses me with a tenderness that has my eyes springing open to gaze into his orbs that are mixed with love and something else I keep seeing on my husband's face. Cain is scared.

"Cain," I whisper into the darkness of the room. I woke up to use the bathroom a few hours after we went to bed, where he proceeded to make love to me slow and tender, to find he was not in bed. I took care of my business and slipped on one of his t-shirts along with a pair of shorts. And now, now I'm standing beside him next to Justice, and her precious little sleeping body curled on her side, her little pink stuffed bunny held tightly to her chest. "I used to dream of having a child with you, what he or she would look like. Talk like. She's nothing like those dreams. She's a reality. She's ours. And I'm going to do everything I can to keep her safe," he whispers.

"I know, honey." The way he shuffles his body behind me, curls his arms around my waist, and places his head on my shoulder to where I feel the warmth of his breath at the shell of my ear tells me he's not done talking, that what he has to say needs to be said in a hushed tone.

"You wanted to kill tonight, didn't you, to rid them of their souls, rip their black hearts out of their chests. And yet you held back?" He nips my ear.

"Yes," I murmur.

"Can you promise me something?" The way he changes the course of this conversation throws me off a little; I still nod in agreement out of curiosity. I would promise him anything. He knows it.

"Don't leave this house until this is over." My body tenses. He feels it, knowing I suspect more to his request. He grips my hand to pull me silently behind him, shutting the door and descending us down the stairs.

"Where are we going?" I startle when I find Roan sitting at the kitchen table with a half-empty bottle of his favorite scotch and a glass in front of him, drained.

"Hey," I murmur softly. I take one step forward as I drop my hand from Cain's. My breath catches in my throat when he lifts his head. His eyes are full of misery, pain, and an indescribable feeling of sadness flashes across his features before he uprights himself out of his slumped position in the chair.

"Roan," I say as my feet paddle sheepishly across the cool hardwood floor. "Someone tell me what's going on, please?" I beg. I've never seen him look this distraught or this beaten down before.

"You should be in bed," he slurs slightly. I ignore him for a moment to pull out a chair and sit beside him. Cain takes one across the table. I glance from him back to Roan. I'm confused as to what's going on, how Cain knew he was down here in the first place.

"So should you," I say thoughtfully.

"Yeah, well. I have a lot on my mind. Sleep isn't an option. At least not tonight." He leans back in his chair with his hand clasped behind his neck, diverting his compressed eyes toward the ceiling.

"Tell me. Let me help," I beg.

"You can help me by staying here. After what almost happened tonight, I'm refusing to let any of you leave here. There's no negotiating, Calla. Don't try your courtroom tactics, your pleas, or your bargains on any of us. Put an ease to my fucked-up mind and agree." I am about to argue with him when he turns his head my way, his request replaced with unshed tears.

I now know why I'm here. He's breaking. A chill runs up my spine, stopping short of stabbing me in my skull. Something happened tonight. Something these two weren't going to share with me, but now that I'm up, they have to. No matter how irritated towards both of them I am for telling me to stay put, or what I want to do, this needs to be about him. His needs come first. I'll do whatever it takes to bring back my smart-mouthed, full-of-life cousin. "Okay. I'll do whatever you need of me. Just talk to me. Tell me what's eating you up." I sense something very wrong here. It's deeper than what happened earlier tonight. Roan has a story that has been killing him. I know it.

"You really want to know?" His voice is getting louder with each emphasized word.

"Only if you want to tell me." I won't pressure him or interrogate him. All I want to do is give him the opportunity to ease his aching heart.

To free his soul from what I can clearly see is ripping him apart.

"It's my dead fucking brother. He's still tormenting me from his grave. Controlling my life. Destroying it in ways I can't fix. Did you know that Hector, the man my dad adored, is a goddamn rat?" I go pale at this news about Hector. The news about Royal isn't something new at all. What in God's name happened tonight? "That's right, a motherfucking traitor to his own brother, his family, just like my brother. He wants this," Roan waves his arms around the massive kitchen. "My life, your life. He wants the Diamond Empire, Calla. So what does he do to try and get it? He sends people to try and kidnap you tonight. To take away another person I love out of my world. There you have it. That is why I can't sleep. Why I'm down here racking my brain over how in the hell I'm going to get away with killing him." A strangled cry leaves my mouth. I begin to shake at this information. Does he want to kill Hector? Oh God, this cannot be happening. My eyes mist with tears for my cousin, who's in so much pain I don't know what to say to help him. He spent his entire childhood being ridiculed, bullied, and almost killed on a few occasions by his brother. Both he and I witnessed first-hand the kind of sick, twisted psychopath he was. I'm speechless at how much hatred is in our world, at the crimes being committed for materialistic reasons. Money? Power? Those are the weapons that lead a person straight to hell, and the kindest man sitting in front of me cares nothing about those things. He cares about the only things that truly matter in life. Family. Love. Happiness.

"Roan, Calla, Cain." I jump from the unexpected voice in the doorway. The two of them tilt their heads as if they were expecting someone else. Anton follows in behind him. Both of them are dressed in black. It's then I notice Cain is too, as well as Roan. My throat constricts. My heart picks up speed. My maze of a mind demands to know what the hell is going on.

"Ivan, what are you doing here?" I stand abruptly the minute they both grace us with their presence to stand at the head of the table. I catch

Roan grab the back of my chair as it tips backward when I push myself up in a hurry.

"Sit back down, Calla. We're all here to help Roan get away with killing Hector."

ROAN

Jesus Christ. I came down here to drain my mind, to clear it for a few silent hours before all hell breaks loose. With the first sip of the brown liquid that burned like a bitch going down my throat, all I could think about was the hell my brother continues to put me through. Somehow, the sick fucker is still tormenting me. His ghost is fucking with my head. Instead of the bourbon flowing through my bloodstream to calm me, it went straight to my heart, pinching off the arteries to a point where I felt my heart crack in my chest.

The more I drank, the more all the memories invaded my mind. The way his face lit up whenever he left me deflated when we were young. The look of a soul-less kidnapper when he injected heroin into Calla. The animosity, bitterness, and no loss of love when he sliced my finger off like he was cutting through a cheap steak. The worst memory of all was the wounded expression on Alina's face when she broke down and confessed he'd raped her all those years ago.

My heart is bleeding out, draining me to the point I can't think straight anymore. I killed a man tonight, came home to my sleeping pregnant wife, who I wanted to hold in my arms, smell her sweet scent. I couldn't do any of it. Not until this goddamn shit is over. Until I've rid myself of my demon brother once and for all.

I knew Cain would be down soon after the group text we received from Aidan, letting us know he found Hector and that he and John would have some fun torturing him until we arrived. Imagine my surprise when Cain walked in with Calla. The moment she saw the booze, my face and my heart lying on the table, I spilled my guts out to her. Told her the truth. Just when a big part of me is relieved to get it off of my chest, in walks Ivan, followed by Anton. John must have called them, because he knows how hard this is going to be for me. They're here for support. Ivan's words flow through my head of how he's going to help. He's already taken care of what needs to be done to thwart Hector's disappearance away from us. I can see it in his eyes, the way he looks at me with a smug tilt of satisfaction across his mouth. He's also ready to go, to get this painful shit over.

"It's two o'clock in the morning. This couldn't wait?" Calla glares at the two of them, bringing me out of my depressed living nightmare. Her expression is turning ice cold. I barely got my words out to her about Hector's betrayal before they walked in. By the look on her face when I told her and the way she is glaring at the two of them with protective armor masking her face, Cain hasn't told her a damn thing about what we found out tonight. I don't know if I should beat his ass or be grateful. It doesn't matter. I would have told her in private the first chance I got anyway.

"Not when we have a PI tied up and gagged on this property." Ivan's statement sobers me up instantly. Calla's eyes go wide. Most of all, I'm thankful they are here to offer their help. Like I told Calla, I have no clue how to off him. He's family. A man I trusted. A traitor to my dad. Now, as I sit here, I'm consumed with fear that I acted on impulse to get him here. That I may have put our lives in danger because of it. Either that, or my ass is about to go to jail if the cocksucker has confided in anyone, if he told them if anything were to happen to him to investigate me.

"Oh, my God. What the hell is going on here? Are you saying that Hector is here? That you have him in the barn? We… you…you can't kill him. He works for the police. He's bound to have evidence stashed somewhere. Records of the work he's done, taped phone conversations, videos. You may as well shoot yourselves if you do this." Calla stands taller, her shaky hands gripping the edge of the table.

"I can and I will. Besides, he's a vindictive son of a bitch. He was involved in the killing of my friend. My confidant. A man like him does not deserve to live. He's gone too far with his greed. He needs to go. And do not underestimate me, young lady. This is not my first time cleaning up the filth from the streets of New York. The minute he stops breathing is the minute his office blows the hell up. His home is being swept for evidence as we speak. His connections are being beaten and burned out of him now." Ivan's anger burst out of him like an erupted volcano as he stands and challenges Calla.

"That's enough." My uncle walks in with his shoulders pulled back and his hands curled into fists. He looks so goddamn tired. His worn face is filled with rage.

"This is the kind of bullshit that will rip us all apart if we don't get control of this. We need to stand united. Calla, Ivan is right. This is what we do, how we conduct business. There are no second chances here. Hector fucked up. He fucked up big. He will pay with his life. You are my daughter, the greatest blessing in my life. That man out there," he points his finger in the direction of the barn, "was going to kidnap you tonight in hopes that Roan would bring him into the Diamond Syndicate. That he could use my daughter as a bargaining chip. Do you know what that means? That means he would have turned you over to the Irish if Roan hadn't cooperated with him. And God forbid where you would end up from there." Jesus Christ. I close my eyes to soak all of this in, opening them only when I hear a sob escape her lips. Tears are running down her cheeks.

"Calla. None of us are trying to scare you. We are giving you the fast version of the stone-cold truth. I know how hard this is for you; you took an oath years ago, knowing you would defend criminals. Then you were thrown into a role you weren't prepared for. A role you haven't had time to let truly sink in, to learn all that goes with it. You are twisted up about this, but you have to stop. Show us the tough woman I know well enough to know she thought about killing those men earlier. The bastards who dared to put your little girl's life in danger. You wanted to gut them, to let them know you will do whatever it takes to protect those you love. Remember this. If we don't kill them, they sure as hell will kill us. And one more thing, sweetheart; what's about to go down right now is mild compared to how this all will end." Uncle John walks forward this time, his shoulders slumped. When he reaches her, he wipes the tears away that are falling like a sudden downpour, bringing her into his arms. I watch her go willingly, sighing as she buries her face into his chest. I feel for her. She's confused, and she should be with everything that is being thrown in our direction all at once. Fuck, if I'm honest and sentimental here, it's the goddamn truth to why I came down here in the first place instead of heading straight out there to end the life of a man I love. It's too much for me to consume. My heart is scattered in tiny fragments over my brother; my mind is worried about Lorenzo, Calla, my family, this empire. I'm a box overloaded with fuses; every single one of them is detecting a fault that's tripping my mind, to lose the spark I need to keep the current coursing through my veins.

The typical no-go zone of telling our women about the lives we take doesn't apply to her anymore. Calla may know what we do, but to hear it spoken out loud is an entirely different story. And her outburst against Ivan only proves to us all how unafraid she is to say what's on her mind. It's her heart she needs to swallow down in one choking gulp. She needs to hear that from me and no one else. My cousin will come into this role with a powerful vengeance now that she knows that no crime, no man is too big or too small for us to rip apart.

My uncle is a man who rarely raises his voice, but… what he said to her she needed to hear. I needed to hear it again. To remind me of what I'm really dealing with: a man who has stepped over the boundaries he was given. He fucked up. Therefore, he must pay.

"I'm sorry." Calla places her hand on my arm. Her compassion for my well-being is as easy to read on her as one of Alex's books. "This has nothing to do with my oath. I wanted to gut whoever was behind that wheel tonight. I came this close," she pinches her thumb and forefinger together, "to walking down to that barn tonight, to beg for you to let me kill. My mom and yours talked me out of it." She angles her head up to stare me in the eyes. "They made me realize that my place isn't down there; it's here doing the work you need me to do. What this means is, if you kill him, the cops will investigate, the Irish will suspect we know. We won't stand a chance in hell of getting Lorenzo into that ring. They'll bring this war to our front door. If that happens, I'm scared for all of you. That some of you may not make it out alive."

Her bloodshot eyes scour each one of us with a depth full of concern. They stop when she looks lovingly into Cain's eyes.

"I'll always come back to you, Calla." His voice is soft, his eyes pleading with her to absorb what he's saying.

Calla needs to understand a few more things before we finish the business my hands are itching to do.

"Don't apologize for caring about us, Calla. For worrying. Every one of us has feelings. Every man in here worries whether today or tomorrow will be the day we die. None of us want to die. But we will if it ensures in any way that we have protected our families. My dad is dead; that man down there played a part in it. He tried to get his hands on you. Trust me when I say he won't be missed by the cops. They know exactly what kind of goddamn snake he is. The only reason someone hasn't killed him yet is that he was under the protection of every fucking fool he's betrayed. So fuck him, fuck the Irish. We may not be invincible, but I'll guarantee the love we have for our families will bring every one of us home alive." Does she get it now? Every damn thing? I don't think she does, not quite yet anyway.

"You caught me down here alone tonight when you walked in here while I was fighting my inner self; you deal with your worries inside your head. There isn't a day that goes by when I wish I could have had a brother who loved me. I never had that. The man didn't know the meaning of the word, not like all of us do here. You have no heart when you kill someone, only a black hole that you bury it in. It resurfaces when you walk through the door to those you love. You may go crazy that way, but trust me when I say it's the only way you'll survive. What I need for you to do now is let this go, go rest, since," I pause briefly since my next words will have her upstairs tossing, turning, and pacing the floor until she knows we're all back. Therefore, I must choose them wisely. "You're right that the minute Donal realizes Hector is missing, he'll become suspicious. Tomorrow, I'm going to need you to work with Dilan and Sandman to make sure word gets to Donal that there is a fighter who is threatening to take down the best man he's got."

"If you feel you can't do this, brother, then let me know?" Cain asks me about a half hour after Calla left us. She didn't blink an eye when I gave her explicit instructions on what she needed to do. It has to be done. Quickly.

"I didn't show mercy to my brother, which means this fucker will be easy," I answer truthfully, then swing open the door to the barn, allowing everyone in before closing and locking it behind me.

"Let me be the one to draw his last breath," Uncle John asks from up ahead. Now that I have the strength built up that my dad meant nothing to this piece of shit, I'm ready to gut him. My entire body craves the desire to stare into his eyes when all of his senses weaken, his pupils dilate, and the last bit of air escapes his lungs. I'll give my uncle the satisfaction of killing him.

"He's all yours to do with what you wish after I let him know exactly what he took from me. Not only do I want his soul to suffer in hell, but I also want his mind to skip like a broken record, repeating my words until the devil himself can't stand to hear him speak and he casts him into the roaring fire of the netherworld." We all laugh as we descend the stairs, open the door, and stop immediately, taking in the sight before us.

"Jesus, John, is the fucker even alive?" Ivan pulls out a cloth to cover his nose from the stench of burning flesh that's vested itself in this room.

"The price you pay for trying to take my daughter. Isn't that right, Hector?" He pulls some gloves out of his pocket, stretching them over his hands before he yanks the already half dead traitor's burnt face in his direction and begins to nod his head up and down for him.

"I thought I'd do the funeral home a favor while you went up to the house. Started cremating the rest of his body. Although, there won't be a body for them to find." Aidan chuckles, like burning the flesh off of someone's skin is an everyday occurrence for him. Crazy fucker.

"I'd love to be able to stay and watch you end this maggot's life. I have a very pregnant wife who I'd like to hold in my arms. He's all yours. Make him suffer." Aidan pats Hector on his head before he tightens the straps around his ankles in what we call the electric chair. It's a solid form of torture. One we use often. Not to persecute by electrocuting them. I must say though, the expressions on their faces when they see the aged chair is priceless. It's the easiest way to have them shitting themselves when they think they're going to die by electrocution. No, a 2000-watt zap to their body is too damn easy. We use it to make sure they are sufficiently strapped down without a chance to escape. To make them suffer.

"Hector," I say with a deep drawl from the hatred I've built for him sifting through my throat like the sweet taste of candy.

"You scared?" He doesn't answer me, only stares me down with the once whites of his eyes that are now a bloodshot red. *You should be, you rat bastard motherfucker.*

"With all the fields you play on I'm sure you know how this goes down. You tell us what we need to know, and I promise you, my uncle over there will kill you quickly. If you don't, I swear on the life of the brother you ratted out to be murdered, I will leave you in here with him for days." To demonstrate I mean what the hell I'm saying, I reach into my pocket and produce an old pocketknife that belonged to my grandfather. It was the one my dad carried around with him everywhere. I watch his charred face contort in anger when I flick open the small blade, twirling it in my hand.

"That should have been mine," he coughs out, voice raspy and dry as a desert.

"I don't think so," I say while watching his mouth snap shut. What's left of it, that is. Half of the top of his lip is burned off. I'm surprised he's still able to talk.

"You wouldn't." He tightens his jaw. The muscles that have to be burning to work overtime in his face twitch when I place the blade up against the denim covering his balls. "I'll slice these bitches off, Uncle," I stress out. The familiar word seems so foreign to me now.

"I've been carrying around guilt for so goddamn long. Guilt that should never have been mine to carry when all along it should have been yours. How long have you been working with Royal, you bastard? That's what you really are, isn't it? A piece of trash who was never wanted. A sick fucker like him. So blinded by greed and distrust that you could never see the love that surrounded your nasty fucking ass. You saw to it, didn't you? You made damn sure my dad suffered for my grandfather's sins. A man who fucking loved you no matter what your name was. He trusted you. I want to know why, when he offered you nothing but his undying love, why in the ever loving fuck would you…"

"He thought the world should revolve around him. Around you, Calla, and Cecily." He looks to John after he cuts me off. Saying my aunt's and my cousin's name in the same sentence has sealed his fate. It won't matter how badly he wants him dead. John is going to make him pay a long-ass time before he reads the expiration date on his life to him. I see veins protruding in my uncle's neck as the bitterness continues to roll off of Hector's tongue like a practiced speech. "Cecily never wanted anything to do with me. She deserted me all those years ago like everyone else when she moved away with you. Left me with a mother who killed herself when I was sixteen years old over a man she could never have. A man who used her for a piece of ass. And I tried, I goddamn tried to be a brother to her when you all came back. But no, she had her head so far up my brother's ass that she never took the time to get to know me. So yes, I set him up. Yes, I wanted to hurt all of you by taking Calla, handing her over to Donal and let him sell her. Make you all pay for losing someone you love. Like this fucked-up royal family who thinks they own this corrupted world did to me." Thankfully, his voice comes through crystal clear this time. No raspy effect. Only words that have me standing, placing my hand over the top of his and slicing through the bones of every one of his fingers. He screams, thrashes against the restrains he will not be free of. I will not give him the satisfaction of knowing the words he spits out effortlessly struck me in the middle of my chest as if he took this knife out of my hands and flung it through the air to dangle as carelessly as the words spitting out of his dry-lipped mouth.

"Tell me what Donal has planned. How the fuck did the two of you get involved with Royal?" I'm inches from his charred face, holding his hand down by the wrist while his blood stains my pants and drops in a pool all over the floor. I want him to bleed the fuck out, feel the pressure in his blood flow bursting his eardrums from beating so goddamn hard in his ears. What's left of the color on his face drains away like a poof of smoke when I lower my knife back to his balls. I'll show him the same mercy he gave my dad: none. I'm not sure how many times I poke through his jeans with the tip of the blade, penetrating the flesh on his balls, blood soaking through his jeans. He's a fucked-up mess. One of the men who tore the heart out of my mom's chest. This will never bring my dad back, but I'll make damn sure there isn't a part of his body that doesn't feel pain so deep he will wish he never inflicted it on others.

"You were family, you filthy cockroach. Family!" I roar. My hands begin to shake uncontrollably, and before I realize what I'm doing, I have it at the base of his throat, ready to cleanse my soul, to have his death on my hands. I watch him intensely as terror itself takes over his face, his shitty life he thinks he had flashing before my very eyes.

"I drove the nail of hate further into Royal's heart, you little shit. An eye for an eye and all that. He was an outcast like me, so the minute I knew he was here, I corrupted him more. Introduced him to the only family I've truly had: the Sweeney's." Christ, I could easily carve out his Adam's apple the way it's bobbing up and down; those nerves of his closing in behind it have to make his throat raw.

"Finish." I press the blade in as far as I can without killing this fucker. My shaky hands are dictating me to do it though.

"Donald took me in when he found me homeless on the street. Took care of me, fed me, and loved me like a brother. Once I knew Royal trusted me, I introduced him to Donal, Jr. You can figure out the rest. I'm done talking.

"The fuck you are. You spit it out." My hand is slipping. I'm going to sever his cords in a second.

"They promised to kill each other's dads, man. They wanted it all. I've been a goddamn pawn since. Biding my time until Donal killed me off. So there you go, you all are only doing him a favor." My eyes go wide, my entire body shaking with uncontrollable tremors.

"Roan, stop." Cain grabs my wrist, my head inclining in his direction. The fog is slowly lifting from my vision. "Get out of here," he quietly instructs.

I hear Cain, yet I don't. Hector's words are all on repeat as they sink into my bones. The biggest form of unfaithfulness will be rotting right next to my so-called brother. They both kill each other's fathers? Jesus Christ.

I pull my hand back and wipe the blood from the knife on my jeans while I'm shaking my head to the unbelievable shit I'm hearing.

"Fuck off, you little punk. You'll never be man enough to run this empire if you can't even kill me yourself. They'll all destroy you." He's wheezing now, the agony he's in selling him out in his tone.

"They," I say on a maddening grunt. "You mean, as in Donal and Sergei, or are there more?" I run my suspicions by him. His words have everyone silenced in this damp room that smells like death.

"Sergei? No. Even though I hate the fucker, he doesn't have a thing to do with this. The only thing he wants is more money than he can spend, and his limited amount of pussy. Keep him away from your wives. It's funny how he and I want something we both know we will never have." I never tear my gaze away from him, and yet I feel Cain tense up from his confession over what we already knew about Sergei's way with women. If he's telling the truth, then maybe Sergei isn't in with them after all.

"I'm talking about the Irish. Donal. His team," he screams. I'm slowly swaying backward, the need to regain control weighing heavily on my body. I need to get the fuck out of here, so I can happily rid myself from looking at this toxic waste that's creeping into my veins to where it has my heart out of rhythm, my mind unfocused, and my life in a whirlwind, my glazed-over eyes not once leaving my dead uncle's until I slam the door behind me.

"They're coming for you. You will have nothing but a stiff, dead body like mine when they are done with you. That's the way Royal wanted it. He's going to get his wish. To ruin you all. To leave you with nothing like you all did to both him and me."

It all makes sense. Why Hector and Royal hooked up. And I know…
I know without a doubt that's how they sunk their teeth into the
Sweeney's. Consuming them with lies about us. How we can't be
trusted, how we outcast our blood. Loyalty is the one thing we all
demand. Royal showed it to Donal, who thinks we outcasted our flesh
and blood. This fucker here, he needed to keep the information rolling
in about us. That's how they knew where my dad would be that night.
He told them. This son of a bitch had them nourishing off of everything
they knew about us, feeding it to an enemy who could have easily
become an ally.

Sweat beats down my spine. My vision blurs. I need to get the fuck
out of here before I take the honor away by demanding I kill this bastard
myself.

"You make sure he told us everything. Then feed his corpse to the
sharks." In less than thirty seconds, I slump outside the door, my ass
hitting the cold cement floor. I stay in a state of shock, hurt, and
confusion, repeating his words of them coming for us in my head. I have
to derive a plan. Get to them first. "Motherfucker!" I yell over the top
of his screaming, his begging for them to stop. Their deep voices are
ignoring his pleas of bargaining. It's not until I hear my uncle ask him
if he knows what Donal's next move is that I become utterly still, when
my shaky hands that are now cradling my head stop.

"I don't know what he plans next. What I do know for sure is, he
wants both Calla and Roan dead."

CALLA

"Is he dead?" My God, I sound maliciously sadistic and uncaring. Asking that question leaves a bitter taste in my mouth and a palm that burns as if I've slapped Roan myself for asking. He cared for Hector, in a way he cared for his brother too, and they both tore the man's heart out of his chest. Two members of your family out to destroy a person in ways that should make you lose your mind, give up, yet here Roan went down there to face the man. To perform his job to protect the rest of us from these hideous men.

I study my husband, who looks well past exhausted when he enters our room. The sun is rising high in the sky, letting me know it's close to noon. Its warmth is beating on my face. I've been sitting in front of the window for hours, staring into the direction of the barn, while Deidre entertained my daughter. I'm unable to move for reasons I can't explain. Hurt, fear, and a feeling settled in the pit of my stomach that more has gone on out there than the killing of a man who deserved to die.

The dark sky slowly turned to dawn, obstructing my view from being able to see a thing outside as I barely breathed air in my lungs until I saw all of them walking up to the house with their heads held high and their strides set in determination. Well, I'm determined too. The whole time I've been sitting here with my mind bantering back and forth between what's happening out there and what I can do to make this all come to an end. I want to take charge of the destruction of the sick sons of bitches who have put us all here. Thus, I've made a decision. One that none of them will agree with. Especially the man I love. I'm tired of it all. I will not tolerate a man with no heart to control the beating of my own anymore. Nor will he destroy us. And he wants to; he wants to bring us down. Well, fuck that. I'm not going to sit still on his pendulum any longer. I'm ready to soar, to swing freely.

It's time for me to do what I need to pull this family back together. My reason is justifiable. This is my family. Mine. It doesn't have a thing to do with them torturing a man while I imagined it, craved it, and now I need it. Hector deserved all he received throughout the morning hours in a place that felt far away when in reality, his death lied over the tops of the green foliage of the trees. I listened to his screams, wished for them even, and I felt nothing. And now I feel everything that life has to offer me. Pain, anger, fear, love, lust, and the urge to vomit from them all for what I'm about to say now that Cain is here.

My skin is stocked with a coat of sweat under the wool blanket I have wrapped around me. I never pulled it off of me after my body chilled, my brain freezing up then thawing out when my plan sprung into my head. Everything soaked into my skin like a burn from all I discovered in the past twenty-four hours. This is an absolute mess. Lives are being taken. And the scariest part of it all is, I really don't care about any of those deaths. What I do care about are these men taking a chance of losing their lives by continuing to wear themselves down with meetings, phone calls, being away from their families. I ache for regularity, long to live, and by God, I'm going to make it happen.

After hearing everything tonight, from Ivan's declarations to the wise information from my dad, most importantly the news Roan shared, I hope to God they haven't left a part of Hector unmarked. He deserves every damn thing they've done to him. His torrid affair in his fucked-up mind between love, hate, and what's right and wrong is a disaster to my family. He committed treachery in its finest form that now I hope he suffered in ways he will never comprehend.

"He is." The love of my life speaks in a low, strained way that has me on high alert as I survey his rugged, handsome features.

His hair is still wet from the shower he always takes before he returns home after they have killed someone. Only this time, his face doesn't show the peace that normally follows. This time, he's angered even more than before he left.

"Cain. What happened?" I stand, my heart hitting the floor right along with my feet. All I can think is something went terribly wrong. I need him to tell me before I crumble him to the ground by swaying him in a direction he's liable to strangle me for.

"Hector said they're coming for us. He doesn't know when or how, but," he hesitates for a moment, causing my nerve endings to flare, "they're coming, and he wants both you and Roan dead. That's not all either." His words trip my mind like a livewire. Hearing those words makes me realize I'm right in my thoughts. The phone call I recently made to a man I can't stand and who agreed with me told me those same words.

"What else?" I whisper.

That livewire sets off the explosives after he tells me what was said out there. It underlines my determination to do what I have to do even more. Roan has been through enough. It's time those of us who truly love him stand up for him for once.

I toss the blanket off of me, stand abruptly, and swallow the terror his eyes are boring into mine.

"They won't get me if I get them first," I say while approaching him slowly.

"What? You're not making any sense, Calla. You planning on killing Donal yourself? Is that what you're trying to say?" He laughs lightly, then stops abruptly. He knows I'm not joking around. My voice is hazardous when I speak next.

"That's exactly what I'm saying. I have a plan. One that will get me inside to sit in on that fight. If what Hector said is true, then we are in worse shape than we thought we were." Cain takes a step back away from me. I bite my tongue, waiting, anticipating for him to verbally attack me. To tell me I've lost my mind. I'm shocked when he says nothing about what I said right away. I can see the wheels in his head spinning out of control. His temper is flaring. He's ready to crash. I'm not going to let that happen. He is not going to try and strip this from me. I go to say just that when he cuts me off with the sharp bite of his tongue.

"I'll lock you in this goddamn bedroom if you even try to leave here. You fucking get me, Calla? And one more thing," he hesitates, then wipes his hands down his weary face. I can tell by his tense shoulders and his hard glare when he raises his head to look at me that I'm not going to like what I'm about to hear. In fact, I'm going to hate it. Hate it as much as he hates trying to say it.

"Roan is trying to derive a plan with Silas to help bring them down," he tells me in a rickety voice that leaves me unsettled.

This unexpected turn has scenes twisting my mind beyond my wildest thoughts, my worst nightmares. I'm not sure what to think, what to say, or how to respond to the vagueness coming out of his mouth. *Silas said he was with me on this.*

"What are you talking about?" I manage to get out, even though I'm afraid to hear. Silas better not be fucking us around. I probed that son of a bitch on the phone harder than he did me in the meeting. I point blank asked him if he had anything to do with my uncle's death. His sudden gasp in my ear gave me the truth before he spoke it. He had nothing to do with it.

"I'm a man of my word," he had said. "I want them out of this country as much as you do. I'll do anything to help." Little did he know the help I was asking for included the possibility that my husband may kill him first.

Cain scoffs. His next words cut me more. "How the hell do you think you're going to get inside? By showing up on someone else's arm? Pretend like you and I are split up? There's not a chance in hell they would believe…" Displeasure flashes in his eyes while mine narrow at the mere thought that he guessed my plan right.

"You have lost your goddamn mind if you think I will ever allow such a thing. This is ridiculous. You were told to stay here, to work other angles, to help Dilan, and now all of a sudden it's all changed? You're fucking crazy. Not only that, you're plotting your goddamn death. I'm not listening to this bullshit. You've pushed this as far as it will go. Don't bring this up again. The answer is fucking no, Calla. Always no." Tears fill my eyes as I stand here and watch the man I love try and tear me down. He will not waver the confidence I have built all night long while plotting this.

Something clicks in my brain as we stand only a few feet apart, his chest heaving, his hands clenched. It sends a biting force through my veins that nearly freezes my blood flow. He knows I'm right. I'm the only one of us Donal would believe turned her back on her family. All because I'm a woman who would undoubtedly disagree, argue, create drama, disobey. I'm Lady Liberty. The one who stands proud, tall, and takes no shit. If I disparaged myself from my family, my daughter included, they'd get rid of me the same way he believes they did Royal. The same way they wouldn't fully accept Hector. In other words, he needs to believe I've betrayed them. And what better way than to sleep with the enemy?

"Oh, my God. You know I'm right, don't you. You just won't admit it?" I throw my hands in the air. It's the truth. He knows damn well it is.

"It's never going to work. He won't buy it. Anyone who knows you and me won't believe we are split up. You'll be walking into a death trap, Calla!" he yells. I fight back my tears. The things I need to say are too hard to spit out, too much for me to deal with when all I want to do is climb into bed and curl tight against the only man I love.

"I agree to nothing. Do you really think I want another man to lay one finger on you? Whether it's for show or not, do you think I can just stand by, not knowing where in the hell you are or if I'm going to get a call that informs me you're dead? You have an hour to get ready. Silas is on his way out here. The kids are all sitting down for lunch. I'm going down to eat with our daughter." He turns and walks away, leaving me with questions unanswered. I choke back the sobs I'm desperate to let escape. The confusion and uneasiness linger in our room after he slams the door shut hard enough to make me jump. I'm not sure what the hell is going on here. I'm confused, my thoughts blowing up my brain, my agony deflating my heart. What in the hell is going on? And why didn't Silas call me and tell me Roan contacted him?

Well, good, I think to myself as I slam the bathroom door. They can all find out at the same time that Silas is the man I'm leaving here with.

"She's lost her mind." I hear my mom say just as I'm ready to enter the office. I push the door open without knocking. Time is of the utmost essence here. I'm not about to waste it by standing outside while they talk about me. I'd rather get this over with, let them say all they need to my face.

"I'm doing this," I ground out the moment I walk through the door. I've showered and checked on Justice, who was watching a movie with Anna, Alina, and all of the other kids. Deidre was nowhere in sight. I know she's close to delivering their baby. The poor woman is miserable with swollen feet and all. I didn't ask about her when I spoke to my dear friends for a moment. I guessed she was taking a nap. The four of us are close. We have been since we've all known one another. I'm doing this for them too, my sisters, my friends.

"You know, don't you?" I fished out carefully. I needed to know if they too thought I was crazy. The women I love looked at me like they felt sorry for me. I'm making myself the pawn that's delivered to evil to save their lives and possibly lose my own.

"How can we not?" Anna tilted her head toward the angry voices of my husband and mom coming from down the hall. I wanted to talk to the girls, and yet I knew I had to get in there. I told them I would talk to them soon, thanked them for keeping an eye on Justice, and now here I am.

Every muscle in my jaw is now twitching as I take a hard glance around the room. My knees buckle instantly when I see that everyone is in here. My mom, my mother-in-law, Dad, and the slimeball himself who better protect those balls if he's fucking me over. Silas. I give him the hardest stare of all, telling him if he knows what's good for him, he will not double cross me on this.

"Calla, you need to listen. There isn't a single one of us in this room who wants you anywhere near this." My expression hardens from the difference of opinion coming from my mother. I look to Cain, who has his elbows resting on his knees, his head in his hands. Then to my dad, who stands there stoically, his eyes full of understanding. My aunt, who is seated next to my mom, mirroring her sister's expression, except I detect a glint of hope in her eyes. Hope I can pull this off. That I can somehow get inside, lure this crazy man somewhere so these men can get him. I want nothing more than to ask them all if Roan told them about the sadistic plan Royal and Donal made to kill each other's fathers. I don't say a word out of a promise I made never to tell my aunt about her son's involvement in this. Not when she's looking at me like I'm the only chance we have to end this living nightmare as soon as possible.

I remember seeing the wrath my husband tried to suspend on me when I first strolled up to his club, asking for a divorce, years ago. I'm also envisioning my parents, how they forbid me to date a boy whose father they despised. I see Roan, who never told me he was my cousin until I came back asking for the divorce I never truly wanted. The only ones who haven't somehow managed to manipulate me in one way or another are Dilan and Aidan, but they sure as hell are now. Except, Dilan isn't here. My guess is he's out working behind the scenes to get Lorenzo noticed, still. If this is true, at least someone in this family is doing their job. And where is Ivan? His sons? Why aren't they here scheming up a plan with everyone else?

"We're all here to come up with a plan, correct? Well, let's hear it. What have you all decided we should do?" Everyone is still as stone, shocked at my outburst. "You don't have one, do you? You've been down here discussing mine. You know I'm right, don't you?" This has Cain snapping his low-slung head up. His tortured gaze locks with mine. I would much rather be locking my hands around his neck and kissing his lips than be standing here with him so beaten down with eyes that are pleading with me not to do this.

"This is crazy; you know that, right? You could wind up killed." Roan stands from behind his desk. That slap I thought about earlier he just verbally delivered himself. He's weary, drained. Mentally, physically, and emotionally exhausted. His weariness is showing in the way he focuses his tired, dulled eyes on me. He's the boss, so goddamn what? That does not give him or anyone in this room the right to discuss this without me being present.

"Sit down and let's talk about this reasonably, Calla." Cain extends his hand to me from his spot on the couch. His begging me to sit lingers in the air until he drops his hand and grips the chair's arms. I refuse to go to him, not before I say what I've repeated in my head the entire time I was getting ready to come down here. I may never go to him again.

Well, that's farfetched. I'll go to him in an instant, just not now. I love him, the hardass and stubborn man. I know this is killing him.

"I will not sit down. I will not submit to any of you. Before you left here, you expressed very sternly how I was to stay here, away from the danger. Well, danger came to this property last night. It almost ran us off the road. I will not stand by and take it anymore. I am going with him. I'm doing this. You can all support me, and we can sit down and talk about this like the strong family we are, or you can choose to let me walk out of here and handle it my way. The choice is yours." I point to Silas, so they know whom I'm talking about. He doesn't have the look on his face he did the night I met him. He looks as saddened and tormented as everyone else. Conflicted even.

"What the fuck? You are not going anywhere with him!"

"I am, Cain. You said so yourself. He had nothing to do with it, that Roan wanted to work with him. I'm not going to be killed. He's not going to inappropriately touch me, and do you know why? He's why." I point to my beloved father, who I watch flinch for the first time at my explosive sound that has my mom standing up, my husband drawing himself out of the chair. "Of all the people in here, that man will be somewhere in the shadows. No one will lay a hand on me." I fume with a startled cry that escapes from the confines of my raw throat. We're arguing when we need to come together.

Both Cain and my mom reach for me when I stumble back. I hold my hands in the air, warding them off while ignoring their pained expressions. "Now is not the time to coddle your daughter, Mother! And it sure as hell isn't your place right now to try and soothe your wife!" I scream at them. I have never been so furious.

"Goddamn it, Calla! I'm afraid. Don't you see that? You all out there alone. This is crazy, baby," Cain pleads.

"Do you think that when you're gone days at a time, that it's easy for me? That I want you out of my sight, away from Justice? They are coming for us, Cain. You said so yourself. We don't know when, how, or what they have planned. But for fuck's sake, I need you all to let me do this. I'm all we have. And I will not be alone." Those last few words have Roan steepling his fingers under his chin. He's thinking. I'm pleading. My anger is still there, but it halts. It's replaced victoriously with some irreplaceable sense of loyalty. He's smirking. "I'm all we've got, Roan. We can do this. We can."

"Do you trust me, Cain?" Dad interrupts my stare down with Roan. I can't hold back the way he professes his question in a hurtful tone. Is this his way of trying to let everyone know he's on my side? That I know he would never let me leave here without knowing my every move, my every whereabouts? Even so, it crushes me to hear him ask that. I stand there, frozen, watching him with the love I've held for my savior my entire life. My mind is consumed with fury, with emotions escalated so high, that I press a hand over my stomach to calm the queasiness that presents itself with the rage I feel inside. I've trusted him my entire life. And now, I'm devastated to hear those stinging words escape his mouth even if they're meant for someone else.

"Yes. Your question isn't about trust though, is it, John? You're going to help her?" Cain admits what I know to be true by watching the way my dad looks at me with his fatherly pride. He's going to help me. He knows it's the best shot we have.

"John, no." My mom shakes her head. Her denial to believe him is readable as she flashes her anger towards him.

"You and I will talk later, Cecily." He dismisses her without a wayward glance. He then turns his attention back to Cain.

"Cain," he says his name with a heavy sigh. "Trust me when I say I understand how you feel. Trust me when I tell you that what you said is right. She will be in danger. I know her and so do all of you. You also know me. I would die before I let anything happen to the daughter who stole my heart away from me the first time I laid my scarred eyes on her. If any of you think for one second that I won't be hiding in the shadows like she says, somewhere ready to kill the first person who dares to even look at her, then you don't know me at all. I trust my courageous daughter, who took off on her own years ago without knowing her life was in danger the entire time. We all protected her then without her knowing it. We will protect her now. Listen to what she has to say." His eyes hunt mine the same way mine hunt his. Searching, seeking for the bond that holds this family together. I see it within him instantly. How he recognizes it within me beats the hell out of me when doubt clouds my judgment of the woman I am, but he does. It's written all over his face. He trusts me to do this, to save us all.

"I'm scared to do this," I admit to them all.

"Then don't do it. I'll do it."

"The hell you will," my dad says adamantly to my mom.

"Enough!" That one word coming from my aunt solidifies this entire room. I can't help it when my lips twitch at the way she looks at each one of us with the same degree of contempt equal to that of a judge whose courtroom is out of control. Every last one of us she swings a cold, hard look at, even Aidan, who is leaning into the wall, his arms folded firmly across his chest, his legs crossed. He hasn't said a word, and yet she still glares at him like he's been raising his voice with the rest of us.

"We don't fight like this, not ever. My husband deserves peace, and not one of you is giving it to him with the way you're at each other's throats right now. You all would have been stopped before you started if he were here. He's not though, is he? Isn't he the reason why we're all trying to figure out what in the hell to do? It's his name, his blood we want revenge for. Him! I want this ended. I want that man's name that is tearing my family apart out of my house, out of my family, and I never want to hear you speak of him again. Now, every damn one of you listen to me. I'm saying this once. There isn't a right or a wrong way to go about this, but we have to let her go. We have to listen to what she has to say." My heart shatters into a million pieces at her crackling pitch, the tears that stream down her face. Guilt catches the tiny knob in my throat, making it hard for me to swallow when I stand there and watch Roan go to her, pulling her trembling frame into his body.

She's right about it all. Our family is falling apart.

ROAN

It's been twelve hours of pure living hell since I heard the last scream rip from that bastard's dying throat. Hector is gone. Now to get rid of the leader.

I planned on asking Silas for his help when I called him out here after I gave him a test of my own to find out if he can be trusted. Little did I know the meeting I had asked for was going to blow up in my face. That Calla was the one who detonated the bomb.

"Roan, if I may?" Silas speaks so goddamn politely. Everything about him is entirely professional, not at all like the man from the other day who tried to beat Calla into submission with his threats and his questions that had her challenging him right back. I watch him like a hawk as I place his body in the direction where I'm rooted to the spot after my mom left. Her parting words are still buzzing in my ears.

"By all means." I approach him, this time choosing to stand in front of my desk instead of behind it, where I feel isolated to the point I'm drowning in my sweat.

I nod, wondering what this man thinks he has to add to this disastrous situation. If he's going to stick with this plan he's obviously constructed with Calla or if he's going to run out of here and let the entire world know that my family is on the verge of destroying ourselves. That I have no control over what is done or said around here.

"Calla called me early this morning. Her idea may not be planned out down to every detail; however, I agree with her. I didn't come out here to discuss a new plan with any of you, not when the one she presented to me only needs tweaking to make it perfect."

"Perfect to who? You?" Cain snaps. He needs to shut his goddamn mouth before all hell breaks loose again.

"Cain." Calla finally pulls her head out of her ass and places her hand on his chest as she speaks softly to her husband, who needs to listen for once in his life.

"You're letting jealousy cloud your judgment. Please, let him finish." It's in that instant Aunt Cecily lets herself back in after taking my mom upstairs. Dilan, Ivan, Anton, and Sandman are with her. I wonder if she's filled them in on this preposterous idea that has me feeling like my balls are being pulled tight in an unpleasant way. I realize she has when Ivan's eyes show me his understanding that the choice I have to make is one that could destroy our entire world, leaving us with no chance of recovery if I make the wrong move, if we have to wave the white flag in surrender due to the possibility we won't survive if anything were to happen to another one of our own.

Silas starts to speak again, bringing me back to where I need to be. To focus on each word that comes out of his mouth.

"I came out here to tell you all how brave of a woman you have here. One I didn't give the respect to the other night when she rightfully deserves it. Whatever all of you think you know of me, it's most likely true. One thing I'm not is a man who would take advantage of a woman who belongs to another; and I would never taint the memory of

Salvatore Diamond. He was a good man, faithful, and a man of his word. Today, I'm giving all of you my word that Calla will be protected by my men and me. I will return her home safe to you, Cain. That's a promise." His words stun me. I believe they do everyone else too.

"Have you thought all of this through, Calla? Trust me when I say there is the possibility you may be targeted no matter what. You being out in the open will make it easy on him. He could shoot you in the middle of that fight without anyone knowing. Is this a risk you're willing to take? To leave your child? Your husband? Me? Your dad? Are you prepared to kill someone if you have to? Because I recall just last evening when both your aunt and I told you that killing someone, to have blood on your hands, is not an easy thing to live with." Calla's face hardens after she listens to the calming way Aunt Cecily asks the questions the rest of us want answered. Except, she straightens her spine. She stands tall unlike the rest of us at the moment.

"I know what's at stake here, Mom. This has gone on long enough. We are backed into a corner, packed in so tight that none of us can breathe. Look at what he's done to us. We can't go home. We can't live our lives. I can't even register your granddaughter for school out of fear that once it starts, she will be taken from us. So yes, I'm prepared. I want this nightmare to end. If you or anyone else has a better way of doing that, then tell me. Otherwise, we need to sit down rationally and put our heads together to compile a way to end this." They both shoot me a hard, knowingly glance. The decision is up to me on what they are silently expressing. It will likely be the hardest one I'll have to make, the one that could destroy my sanity. I look intently at my brave cousin, drowning out everyone else's heavy breathing and quiet pleas trying to pull me in the direction they think I should go. Only she's not pleading; her bright eyes are telling me to let her do this that she trusts my judgment, that she trusts me to trust her. The soundless exchange between her and me is all I need to make the choice. My mind is made up.

"Where do we stand with Lorenzo?" I ask Sandman before I tell everyone my decision. My observation remains on Calla. She doesn't recoil; if anything, she stands taller. This woman is ready to battle. To take the confidence she possesses into her hands. To rely on a man she couldn't stand the sight of only a few days ago. Most importantly, her faith she retains deep in her soul that every man in this room will take his last breath to save her, just like she's willing to do for us.

"He's been seen, not by Donal himself, by one of his fleabag motherfuckers. The boy is in. He fights the day after tomorrow," Sandman states proudly.

"What did you tell them about him?" I ask when a plan forms in my head. One that will never arise suspicion on the young man and will also lead to us knowing for sure we can trust Silas since he seems to be in love with the idea of people fucking each other up, killing each other for money inside a cage. "They think his name is Gio Bianchi from Nolita, otherwise known as 'Little Italy.' A gem found in a gym in a borough outside of Manhattan," Sandman says with confidence. I focus on Dilan, who confirms with a nod.

"Good. I have a question for you, Silas, before we plan this out."

"Ask. I have nothing to hide," he tells me flippantly.

"How long have you had your driver?"

"About six months now. He can be trusted, if that's what you're asking." I dart my eyes away from his confused gaze to lift a questioning brow at Sandman, my lips quirking up in the process.

"You feel like getting to know the streets of New York?" I ask knowingly.

"As long as I don't have to call his ass 'sir' I'll do whatever the fuck you need." He smirks and crosses his big, tatted up arms across his chest. Goddamn, the dude is scary.

"You have a new driver now. Temporarily, of course."

143

When a person—or in our case, people—feel trapped, they tend to panic. They feel like they're suffocating to death. The weak tend to want to die, while the strong fight with every goddamn thing they have, because their will to survive outweighs the yearning to die. That is exactly what my cousin has done for us all. Our plan may have holes in it right now, but I guarantee they will be filled with the strongest emotions that exist: grief and anger. I feel it more now than I have before. It's washing me away, tearing me up inside. Destroying me and those I love in ways it shouldn't. Calla was so right when she expressed her views of wanting to live. Those words hit me over the head, stopped my heart when I realized we're all mixing those two emotions together. The rage inside us all is spiraling out of control over standing on the edge, while someone else forces our hand to jump. She took ahold of that rage, shoved it off the cliff, and positioned her grief that she has to overweigh it all. Grief all of us are feeling is unfair. I couldn't be prouder of her for standing up for what she believes. There isn't an ounce of doubt that she won't prevail.

She let me know that Cain told her what Hector revealed. I've never seen her look at me the way she did at that moment. It wasn't pity or worry; it was pure love I saw looking at me. A family love. Well, and now it's been two hours since she and my uncle walked out our door with bags in their hands, the willpower of a leader evident in every step she took until they climbed in the back of Silas' white SUV. We all stood there watching Silas climb in the front passenger seat and Sandman getting behind the wheel to drive them away with hopes of our plan working, that she comes out without even the tiniest scrape on her brave heart. I have no doubt in my mind she will triumph over this. Especially now that the only way Cain would agree for her to go was if her dad went with her. Of course, I agreed; we all did. He'll stay out of sight until he needs to be seen. The tension in the room disintegrated the second I told them what I was thinking. What better way to have Silas' driver's younger brother be the up and coming star everyone will be talking about? This will get the both of them front and center, where she will be noticed if they believe Lorenzo was brought in by Silas. It also made it much easier to send her away, knowing she's covered from every angle on the inside.

Just another man to protect her in the house of a man who is going to die in two days. Donal has crossed the ethical line with the plan he constructed. He's made killing him a joy for me.

Our job is done here until the fight begins. I'm not thinking of the one that will happen in the ring. I'm referring to the one that we've all been waiting for since the day my dad was killed. The biggest one we've had on our hands to date. To bring these cocksuckers down. To avenge justice. To kill every goddamn one of them.

While Calla was packing, I checked on my mom, who held her own today. Her truthful words will forever remain in the center of my chest. Our family is falling to shit. None of us know when this man will come at us again. The ratty bastard is everywhere all of a sudden, poking and prodding his way into our lives, and I haven't seen his face once. He reminds me of a rodent that burrows itself underground during the day only to tunnel out at night, his clan following to wreak havoc on their enemies. To prey on the innocent. Well, not anymore. The trap is set to catch this fucker. I have no doubt he will walk right into it. And when he does, I'm going to trip the wire, snap his neck and kill him.

I went from my mom to check on my wife. She's not convinced in the slightest this will work. Alina is a tyrant like one I've never seen before. She refuses to talk to her father over this, yet has no issues with telling me how she feels. I loathe hurting her; she's fragile, hormonal, and pregnant.

"Have you gone insane? Th… this reminds me of everything you went through with your own brother. Everything he did to us is happening all over again. The lies, deceit, the betrayal. You're not thinking this through, Roan. You may think you have it all worked out right down to the last second, I've got news for you even the best of plans explode in people's face. I hope you can live with yourself if that happens." I allowed her to go on her rant, to tell me I won't be able to live with myself if this goes wrong. Every damn word she said is the truth. I let her get it out though, let her attack me in ways only she can. When she was done, she bent down, scooped up Alex, and went to our room, slamming the door behind her with a silent 'fuck you' falling from her mouth. I should be up there trying to smooth things over with her, begging her to understand, to see I've untied my hands that have been bound for far too long. But I can't. There are a few more people I need to make sure understand before I spend the evening groveling at the feet of the woman I love.

It wasn't an easy decision for me to make. However, with every stride I take to the back of the house where I know Cain and everyone else is hanging out watching the kids play outside, I know I've made the right choice. Now, as I approach him, I notice his shoulders are slumped and he has a glass of his shitty scotch in his hand. I know I'm either going to drown in his wrath or beg him to understand that nothing is going to happen to the woman he loves.

"She reminds me of Calla when she was young. Never afraid to get her hands dirty or to lend a helping hand. She was always the first girl in her class to offer to help her teacher. Shit, my little girl helped get your cranky ass through school. Defied us by marrying you behind our back. Don't you dare give up on her. She'll be fine, Cain, I promise. John has her, and you need to pull your head out and take care of your daughter until her mother comes back," I hear her say. I have no idea how long the two of them have been talking like this. Whether he recognizes it or not, the guy has a woman next to him who cares about what he's going through. I could kiss my aunt right now, the way she's mothering him, speaking straight from her heart while aiming her truthful words at him. The man has never held on to his control. With her though, he's doing it. He's absorbing her argument. I wait just outside the door, hoping he lets some of his anger out. When he does, I brace my hand on the wall, stopping me from wobbling on my feet.

"Christ, Cecily, I'm not giving up on her. I'm defenseless, that's what I am. Pissed the fuck off that she made this decision on her own, that she walked out of here without her phone, her wedding rings, or me. She even took her photos of the three of us out of her wallet. I love my wife, always put her first. Her safety, happiness, and her health. My issue is, she's shifted the components that keep this ticking," I see him jab a finger in his chest. "She's doing all those things for us, while I'm here without her." And there he is, the man who's always had my back as well as anyone else's. Always. He feels stranded, hurt. He's usually the one by my side whenever we go out on a job, a kill, or simply to hang at the bar. This time, I need him here, while the rest of us take control of the worst blow we've had to deal with, and he will be blinded to the entire thing.

"Oh, Cain. She wanted to take them with her; I told her if she was doing this, then she had to do it right. She had to walk out of this house with the idea lodged in her brain that she wasn't coming back. If she wears the love she possesses on her sleeve, they'll see right through her. Trust me. She did not want to leave those things behind. And she assuredly didn't want to leave you."

I don't miss the unintentional implication that's a jab to my gut as I'm sure it is to his that Calla is in danger. Coming from the woman who raised my cousin into the fearless woman she is, who wanted her child away from the kingdom of hell, I'm surprised she would toss that in his lap. At least she has the guy talking instead of pouring that crap down his throat. The last thing any of us need is a drunk Cain going ballistic. He loves his baby girl, save for the fact they aren't complete unless she is around. He wouldn't think twice of downing that entire bottle to ease the wrenching torment he's feeling inside. Instead of letting the two of them know I'm accidentally eavesdropping, I wait a minute or two before I saunter in and take a seat in the chair next to them, my eyes trained on the kids playing with Anna and Deidre. I wonder how the two of them are holding up through all of this. They haven't seen Aidan or Dilan for more than a few hours in the past couple of days. Nevertheless, they seem happy while they show the kids how to put soil in a large pot to plant the flowers I see resting beside them. Showing them we can be normal, everyday people. That they can be kids. Free as a bird to roam around, laugh, play, and take in all that life has to offer a child. Alex is out there with them now. I'm sure one of them went to get him or Alina brought him down here when I was in the office talking to Sandman and Lorenzo on the phone, then finishing up the details with Ivan, Anton, Dilan, and Aidan before they took off to do what needs to be done.

Now, as I watch part of my family enjoying themselves, my best friend solemn while he nurses his drink, I close my heavy lids and suck in a deep breath to prepare myself for whatever he needs to say to me.

"She's as brave as both her parents. A leader." I point my finger in the direction where Justice is now grasping on to Alex's hands, showing him the proper way to pack the dirt around his tiny little yellow flower he has stuck in the pot.

"And she is a little too bossy for her own good too. Like her mom, don't you think?" He says, so all I do is nod. "I'm helpless here, brother. It's eating me alive, ripping my guts out. The not knowing where she'll be is sinking me into hell. I can't survive without her. And the irony of it all is, I can't do fuck about it. I can't protect her." The struggle in his hurting words causes my mind to conjure up the notion he's now in her shoes. Both of us are. I don't reveal that to him, he already knows it. The struggle, the push and pull of every beat of his heart, every heave of his chest tells me he's stuck in his head. No matter what I try to say to him, Cain is a stubborn motherfucker. He won't listen; he'll stay under until he has her tucked safely in his arms. I've only got one thing to say to him, one thing I want him to know before I try and smooth this chaos that has put a wedge between my wife and me.

"If I could be in her shoes right now, I would be. I'd give my life for her, Cain. I can assure you I'll make sure she comes back to you even if it costs me my life."

"Fuck, man. I know you would. We'd all give our lives to spare each other's. There isn't anything wrong with that. The only thing wrong is my wife was shoved in the position to be the one to sacrifice when she never should be making that choice in the first place. So don't go blaming yourself when the one to blame is the man we'll slaughter."

I go to leave and grip my brother by the shoulder when I stand, not wanting to discuss this any further by addressing my aunt. Her words to Cain a few minutes earlier are enough for me to know she's accepted what's already been done. I halt after a few steps, her parting words stopping me right before I cross the threshold.

"My brother would be proud of both you and Calla, Roan. You have been dealt with a calamity that even he wouldn't have known how to handle. You both made a choice when you took over. That choice was yours to make. The feelings we have don't mean a thing when I sit here and watch the hearts of two of the bravest men I know bleed out. Those hearts need to pump for you both to breathe. I'm speaking about myself too when I say there isn't one of us here who wouldn't give up our life to save one of our own. It's who we are. Who we were bred to be. In spite of my malicious words toward this idea earlier, the decision you made was the right one to let her prove to this family she has the mind of a woman who upholds her choice. She has our love behind her. That in itself is what will bring my daughter home."

"Thank you, Aunt Cecily," I say, then leave them be.

"Jesus Christ," I mutter. I'm crawling up the stairs lethargically; I'm tired, frantically needing the strength behind my love to get me through tonight. Either that, or I need to seriously down a couple of sleeping pills. I need a good night's rest as much as I need her.

"Alina." I slip my arm around her, hugging her close to me. I know she's awake by the way her breath catches when she exhales sharply. She's curled up in a ball on top of the bed. I die inside with every second that ticks by without hearing her voice. She can yell, scream, or do anything she wants as long as I can hear her. It's the silence that's massacring me on the inside to the point where my ability to speak is tangled in with the muteness I'm receiving from her. I need her to fill the last bit of void that's left behind from the declaration I heard before I came up here to clear the air between us. The air that is concentrated heavily, that my lungs are expanding from the craving they need to function. I feel it. The fear she wants me to drink in like an ice-cold glass of water that would normally quench my thirst. Instead, it makes my blood ice over.

I lie there in the dead of silence for I don't know how long. She doesn't move at all until I splay my hand across her stomach, where our baby we haven't even been able to celebrate for more than a few hours is growing. My fingers are stroking across the smooth skin as she sucks in a breath so deep she gasps.

"I'm sorry I yelled at you. I overreacted when you told me. I'm worried. About her and about you. It's taken everything I have not to tell you to stop, to let this go. To take me away from it all. Every time I gain the courage, I back off until the next time, thinking he's fine, he's doing his job, but it's not only a job, is it? It's your life, our life. One I took a vow to support the day I became your wife. It's just... how can you deal with all of this? It's never going to end, is it? We're always going to be looking over our shoulder. And Calla. It has to be driving you out your mind that she's going out on a half broken limb to save us." Shit. I close my eyes, wanting more than she will know to be able to tell her this is the end. That we will finally feel safe. It's never going to happen. I need to tread carefully with her when I answer. Her being this upset is not good for her or the baby.

"You're worried, baby, about us all. I am too. I'm trying my hardest not to show it. Not to grab you, Alex, and everyone else and run to our homes in Florida. Give it all up and never return. We both know I won't. Not in my lifetime anyway. I may not seem like the man you fell in love with right now, but I promise you he's in there. I deal with all of this knowing I have the love of a woman I don't deserve. A woman I can't stand to be mad at me over this. I need you more now than I ever have, Alina. I need the strength only you can provide me with. I'm nothing without you. You hold me together, whether you believe it or not. As far as Calla goes, she's safe. I promise."

CALLA

They say not to worry about something if it isn't going to kill you. That mythical phrase isn't working on me so well right now. I've been cruising the edge of a panic attack ever since Roan finally agreed. The more I think about it, the closer I get to succumbing to the thought in my torrentially blinding downpour of a mind. I've been one nerve shy of loosening them all to the storm that's stirring up inside of me. If I truly think about it, I know it's been subsequently longer than that. I've just been too busy to notice.

The minute I swooped Justice up into my arms to carry her upstairs while I packed was when it hit me full force. Her sad little eyes filling with tears when I told her I had to leave for two sleep nights for work nearly did me in. I don't think there will ever be a look of confusion that will surpass hers. She innocently gutted me. It didn't help with Cain hot on my ass, whispering one second and shouting the next that I'm to stick with my dad the entire time I'm at Silas' home. I hid it then, just like

I'm doing now. Only now, the farther we drive from our safety and into the danger zone, the more my stomach knots, the dizziness hits, and the uncontrollable urge to cry has my heart beating faster and my body beginning to shake. I really feel as if I could die.

"You okay over there, sweetheart?" my dad asks in his comforting way. He's the only reason I'm not flipping my shit right now. Him and the delicate quality of my mom's voice when she came into the bathroom as I was collecting my toiletries. I let those tears tumble out of my sockets in hope that balling my eyes out would make me feel better.

"I feel like I'm letting you do a job that was meant for me," she stated when she came up to me, wrapping one of her arms around me, her head tilted off center so we could catch sight of each other in the mirror. "It's my job as your mother to worry, no matter what you do. I've told you this already. It's also my job to make sure you're prepared in case you find yourself alone." I startled when she lifted up her free hand, a small black leather case gripped tightly. She set it down on the counter and flipped open the lid like it was an everyday occurrence to reveal a shiny semi-automatic pistol.

"Mother," I ridiculed in astonishment. Hell, I knew she has all kinds of guns; she shoots them all the time. Bonding with my dad, she calls it. But this, this was crazy.

"If you're worried about Cain freaking out about this, then don't. He's taken Justice downstairs to play before he found me and demanded I give you one of my guns. So," she drew out, gauging my reaction as she did. Whatever she saw seemed to appease her when a tug on her wicked lips curled upward. "I thought you needed one as well, knew your dad wouldn't let you out of his sight without one. This one holds a special meaning to me. Therefore, it's yours. You need to have this. You see," she picked up the gun, gripping it correctly, and placed it my shaky hand, "this happens to be the gun I made my first kill with. So, my sweet, brave daughter, if you feel like you are out of your dad's eyesight or even if you don't feel safe with Silas, you shoot them right between their legs, then aim for their heart. You don't take a chance when it comes to my daughter's life, do you hear me?" I think my mom wanted to scare the hell out of me. If that was her point, she didn't succeed. She knew it too.

"After talking to you and Aunt—" She cut me off by placing a finger over my lips. I hate it when she does that. It was obvious though she had something she desperately needed to say.

"I know what she told you. She did it to protect you from the guilt you would feel. She doesn't understand what it's like to kill someone. That's not who she is. I'm not saying it's who you are either. What I am saying is, these people will not hesitate at all to kill you, Calla. They will do it in a way that will make the things your dad has done look like a leisurely stroll. You're a woman with no experience up against men who couldn't care less. You'll get a speech from your dad just like this one. The difference between ours is, even though the man knows you're a grown woman, he still sees you as his little girl. He can't be anywhere in the open, and that is killing him. So you, you need to pull this trigger, get blood on your hands if you feel it's the only way you'll survive."

"Calla, did you hear me? What the hell is rambling around in your head? You tell me now." Dad startles the hell out of me. I forget instantly about my mom or the fact her gun is in my purse, loaded and ready. It's been a long time since I've shot a gun. Of course, my mom knew that, therefore she set me straight when she said it's like a certain part of a man's body. You grip it here," she placed my dominant hand around the grip, followed by the other, setting my fingers around the base in a death hold, "and then with one eye, you aim this bitch and hit your target." Our laughter rang out loudly in the bathroom until she abruptly stopped and gathered my face in her hands with tears in her eyes and told me to make sure it counts if I have to use it.

"I'm thinking about Mom," I tell him truthfully. I won't lie to him, not about this. I'm carrying a gun in my purse while I'm crossing over the streets, counties, like I'm on a Sunday afternoon drive.

"If you're worried about us fighting, don't be. We're fine. She's your mother, Calla; she's always protected you without thinking." I see him flick his hand at me as if he's waving off what I said. I glance up at Silas, who has his Bluetooth headset on. His mouth is rattling off a list of commands to someone on the other end. He's not paying a lick of attention to what the two of us are talking about back here. He's conducting his business, completely oblivious he has other people in his mammoth of an SUV. This thing is pimped out, like the pimp he probably is. The guy still gives me the creeps, no matter if he's on our side or not.

I skip thinking about how ugly this vehicle is and reach down to the floor for my purse. My gaze is resting on Sandman, who reassures me with a smile that reaches his eyes through the review mirror that he as well will go through every necessary precaution to keep me from being harmed.

"I want your story someday, Sandman." I haven't forgotten I need to answer my dad. I'm in the mood to tease the guy. He's seems laid back, yet he's not.

"Not much to tell, although I sure as fuck wish I'd had you as a lawyer all those years ago." *Now look who's teasing*, I think to myself.

"Why would you say that?" I blurt out. Curiosity killed that cat and all.

"Woman. You are braver than some of the scariest motherfuckers I've met in prison. Not one of them would strap up their balls and do what you're doing, family or not. You have some damn big lady balls, and that is no goddamn lie. Excuse my language." He exhales on a chuckle. Now I really do want to get to know him. I know enough from both Cain and Roan that he's as loyal as his brother. Our dear friend we lost to another family out to destroy us. I also have caught glimpses of his tattoo that all the other guys have in memory of Jackson and his girlfriend. A tribal design is drawn out by Deidre, very exquisite and memorable.

"I'm married to Cain. Trust me when I say I've heard worse. Although, this is the first anyone has told me I have balls." I laugh.

He attends to the road while I shift my attention back to my patient dad, whom I catch smiling.

"What?" I say, then lift my purse, resting it on the seat between us, opening the mouth of it so Dad can finally see what I'm talking about. He takes a peek inside, softly chuckles, then dips his head in my direction, whispering softly into my ear.

"You mumble when you're nervous; that's what. Don't' be nervous, not when I'm here. I'll do everything I can to make sure you don't have to use that. If by chance you do, you make sure you kill them, Calla. Shoot them in the motherfucking balls. Now, look at your old man and tell me what's really bothering you." My mom was right and wrong about him. His little girl or not, he's telling me to slay someone if I have to. In the balls, no less, exactly like she said.

I want to laugh at how familiar the two of them are, so tuned to what the other one thinks and feels. Cain and I are like that too. I can't think of him right now.

"Fear," I say on a whispered breath that escapes out of nowhere.

"Oh, sweetheart. Fear will never go away. It will live like a creature of habit inside of you. You have to learn how to control it. To let it know that you are in control of your life, your actions, not some demon who wants to possess you. Fear is when you watch your child hurt, when you know there isn't a damn thing you can do to take her pain away, to sit back and let her learn on her own that life throws a record-breaking curve ball at her, and all you can do is stand there and watch it knock her on her ass until she pulls herself up and tackles all over again to squash, beat, and recognize she is stronger than she realizes. That she is brave. A noble soul. What you're feeling isn't fear. It's anger, cruelty, and indignation over the circumstances that put you in this position. If you were fearful, you wouldn't be sitting here doing the bravest thing you've done in your life." He expresses so much with those potent words of his that are like lyrics to my soul, a song with meaning.

"Am I too old to climb in your lap?" I ask doubtfully, knowing full well I am. In one long speech, my adoring father has managed to crush what I thought was fear and replaced it with indignation that combines the other two emotions into a gale of uproar inside of me. Swirling, destroying to upheave the anxiety that's been crashing my insides like a heavy wave.

"I'll hold you anytime you want." And just like a parent, he unlatches his seatbelt and slides to the middle of the seat close enough for me to lay my head on his shoulder. I'm the daughter of this man who has given me the backbone I need to not let fear overtake the courage to finish what I started.

The sun begins to set over the brightly lit skyline; the haziness of the red and orange subdue as they blend in vibrancy with the colors amongst the top of the skyscrapers as we drive through the busy streets of New York City heading toward the Upper East Side, to the Lennox area, to be exact, which is one of the most expensive areas to live in New York. I hate it. It reminds me of the rich, the famous, and the oh so very ugly snobby people who have their heads so far up their asses they would never see things clearly through the shit if they were to walk in the shoes of a person with compassion. I've dealt with these types of people since I moved here. Especially in the building where I worked. I miss my job but not the people who own and work for the other businesses. I could go the rest of my life without seeing their everyday glare because they know who I am and what I did. Many times, I wished I did have a gun stuffed in my purse to wipe the smug look off of the men's faces and shove the barrel of the gun up the women's asses. Although, it wouldn't fit, because their big heads are stuffed up there. Why I'm discerning myself with them is beyond me. That's not true; it's because I hated living here, the busy bustle of the city, the areas of high society where, contrary to what the world expects, danger is rated higher than in Harlem.

"I think you and I should have dinner out tonight," Silas calls out, his head whipping around to confront me. I watch him nonchalantly place his hand over the small speaker of his earpiece while he waits for my response. This is easy for him. He doesn't have a damn thing to lose. Nothing.

"Why so soon? I thought we were waiting until tomorrow for lunch with Lorenzo," I respond, confused. I'm devastated. I wanted to settle into one of the spare bedrooms in his home, use my dad's phone to call Cain and Justice before he settled her in bed for the night. I told him I would.

"It's wise for us to be seen together as much as possible. My contact has told me Donal is having dinner as we speak at a small Italian restaurant a few blocks from my home."

"I see." I look away from his heating glare. He wants an answer. Impatient prick.

"You look fine. And calm your jittering nerves. We won't be alone. Sandman is going to drop us off out front then park. Let's push this envelope, make this shit look as real as it can get," he says when I glance down to my navy pin-striped capris, my sleeveless red silk shirt, and my red pumps. Those sickening feelings return once again. My throat wants to swallow itself down to the pit of my stomach. This is really happening, and way faster than I thought it would. Good Lord, I'm sticking myself with a rainbow-colored voodoo doll. The pinpricks are controlling my mind. I need whatever colors are prominent for confidence and psychic evaluation. The one for healing as well, because this corrupted lifestyle is going to kill me yet and I haven't even started.

"I... are you sure he's there?"

"I'm as positive as I know for sure I'm riding in this vehicle." I give him the now-is-not-the-time-to-make-a-joke look. A corny ass joke too. This vehicle is god-awful. I feel sorry for Sandman having to drive around the next couple of days with a pair of fluorescent hot-pink dice dangling from the mirror. Talk about someone with balls.

He nods to himself, then speaks into his phone, telling them we will be there in less than a half hour before he carries on a conversation with Sandman on how to get to his home.

"I won't let you out of my sight. You can do this, do you hear me?" My dad startles me when he grips my hand. It's hard to tell if my dad's words are sinking in through the haze my head is in. God, I'm about to go in and pretend I'm this man's new lover. It's simply too late to think about him touching me, possibly kissing me in public.

"I know," I say pathetically. I do know he won't take his eyes away from me, not for anything. It's everything else that's twisting me inside to where every vital organ feels like it's searching for room to function. They're all melting together.

"Take this. It's a burner phone. We have a million of these things. You call me if you feel threatened in any way. I don't care if an eighty-year-old man is looking at you funny or if you feel off. You call me. The only thing you drink is wine, wine from a bottle you watch the waitress open. And don't you get up from that table. Not for anything." Anxiety explodes inside of me, and when it does, I feel an eruption of an out-of-control rage that has me shivering with a sense of pure evil. The unpleasant smell of a revolting man will soon be in my presence; it's enough to make me want to kill him in the middle of the restaurant. To have the courage to walk up to him and slice his throat while I look into his eyes until they glaze over with an empty hollowness while his dark soul slips to the bottom of that fiery well to hell.

"I won't," I say then toss the phone in my purse. The barrel of the gun is taunting me as I hear the phone lightly clink against it.

"You remember why you're in there, and you'll come out the same brave, courageous woman as the one who walked in. You do your job, and I'll do mine." He places a kiss on my cheek before he climbs clumsily into the back, ducking his head out of sight.

As we pull along the curb to the restaurant, I realize why my thoughts drifted to the people who live here in this area, the other lawyers from different firms in the building I worked at. Subconsciously, I knew why. I'm about to commit career suicide when I enter on the arm of another man. I will never be taken seriously again in a courtroom. I will be ridiculed, called names, my face will be plastered all over the Internet and possibly in the papers by morning. I will no longer be labeled Lady Liberty. They will label me as a deserter, a cheat, a despicable piece of shit who fucked over her family when they were down, who left her four-year-old daughter for another man. *Do I really fucking care what they think of me?*

I don't care about any of those shallow people. All I do care about is what my husband will do when he finds out. Except, do I really? If I can deal with pretending, than so can he. He trusts me as much as I trust him. He's scared; well, so am I, but I'm done placating myself, worrying until I'm sick. If I rewind to today, the past week, the past month, all we've been doing is functioning; we get up, we eat, we argue. To most families, that would seem normal, but not to me, not to my family. Not when I'm reliving the numb, empty look on everyone's face in my mind. The vacancy in their eyes that's been there since the day a part of our lives died. And to think the word 'balls' is partly why I'm steaming up inside, to realize just how badly my family is falling apart. If the shoe didn't fit, this would be funny as hell. Although, the shoe fits perfectly. In fact, it fits so well, I'm going to own this meeting with a vengeance. I'm going to make that prick notice me, name-calling or not. That man is going to want me in a bed he will never get me into before he tries to kill me. I'll make sure of it.

"I'm ready," I say with interest. I've deterred all negative thoughts down an endless, dusty road. Positivity has taken over. Hatred has consumed me. This stranger started a war with a family that thrives on love, protection, and a mindset of dependability on one another. I'm going to bust it all to hell, all for a piece of shit who crawled under our solid foundation and cracked it, leaving us no choice but to rebuild.

"I love you, sweetheart," Dad calls out before we come to a complete stop at a stoplight. Before I can answer, the back door swings open, slams shut, and just like that, he's gone. I swallow.

"Everything I say and do is for show, Calla. I won't touch you inappropriately or kiss you where I shouldn't. But I'm going to show you affection, adoration, and look into your eyes like you're truly mine." An extremely harsh breath escapes my constricted lungs. Here I am, grasping ahold of the hand of a man I forced us all to trust, a man who seems to have a different woman on his arm at all times. Funny thing is, I'm going to give them a show in here without a care in the world that my reputation is drowning in the Hudson River.

"Keep up with me, Silas," I say when we enter the dimly-lit restaurant. "If we're going to convince them I've switched teams, that I'm acting like a single woman instead of married, then I'll be the one doing more show than tell. You better not fuck me over either, or I swear on my uncle's grave I will cut your balls off. Agree?"

"I will never agree to have my balls cut off, but I'll agree to you being brave." He winks.

I look up to him as Sandman drives away. My gaze starts piercing then is replaced instantly with a softening look of seduction. My fingers walk up his chest. When I reach the exposed skin on his neck, I let my hand slide around and bring my face to his ear.

"He's watching. Right there in the front window."

"Very well then." Silas grabs my hand, jerks me into his body, and tips my head back to expose my skin. I feel sick being on display like this, ready to vomit when he places a kiss at the base of my throat. I can feel that seedy little prick's eyes bulging out of his head.

"Shall we, my love?"

"Yes. Let's go to war, dear." And it is. I'm stopping at nothing to make sure we win.

ROAN

"Fuck," I hiss out in my dream. Wherever my mind started when I fell asleep shortly after Alina and I talked, it sure wasn't to wake up in a damp sweat with my wife's lips wrapped around my cock or the way her silky hair feels as it moves across my heated skin with every up and down movement she makes.

"I know you're awake," she whispers in the dark.

"Hell, yeah, I am. You know that's one of my favorite things to see." I clear my groggy throat. I'd been so damn tired I could barely keep my eyes open. I swear to Christ I was out before she left the bedroom earlier, mumbling something about dinner.

I flick on the bedside light for my own selfish reasons. My cock gets hard whenever I think about her; he turns into the hardest muscle known to man when she takes him in her mouth. She's fucking wicked with that tongue.

Out of habit, I lower a hand and begin stroking her hair until I reach the end, where I give it a slight tug. Everything about her face takes my breath away the minute our eyes catch. Her hollowed-in cheeks, her wet lips, her eyes that are heated into a blaze of want, all of it is for me.

"Damn, baby. You want it, then get that mouth back over my dick." I'm horny as a motherfucker now.

When I said I needed her earlier, this was the farthest thing from my mind. My wife, on the other hand, has her own way to ease the tension out of my body. Only this isn't something new; in fact, this is Alina at her finest. Alina, who takes control and knows me well enough to break me when she strikes the mood to take things her way.

The way she regards me with a slight tilt of her head, her pupils dilated to match the blackened sky, gives her away. My wife wants to fuck me. I don't care how tired I am. When Alina Diamond initiates one of her fuck sessions, I'm wide the hell awake.

"You bossing me around?" She takes one long lick up the backside of my dick, teasing the tip, then conquering only the head with her mouth. Many times, my sexy wife has done this to me, only to be rewarded with the hard pounding to her pussy she wants. I'll go all night if my horny little pregnant lover wants it.

"Nah. But if you don't take him all the way in, I'll tie you down, spank your ass, and finger fuck you over and over until you're ready to come. Thing is, I won't let you come." I'm pushing my luck here. She knows as well as I do I'm full of shit. There isn't a part of my body that would enter her without wanting to feel, to taste, and to smell her pussy when she comes. She's a divine attraction, a delectable piece of rarity, and she is mine.

"Mmm," she moans around my shaft, her lips opening wide, her jaw flexing as she begins her slow torture up and down. Mix in her little whimpers of pleasure and her lips, mouth, and tongue, and I'm ready to blow after a few minutes of her tortuous assault on my dick.

"Get up here, baby."

"Maybe I don't want to," she says around another lick. Fuck that.

She may hold all the power at the moment, except she fails to forget I know how wet she is, and I'll be damned if I don't want that wetness gliding across my stomach while she slides her sexy ass up here. As much as I love her mouth, I love her pussy more, and my dick needs to be inside of her right the fuck now.

"Too bad." I let go of her hair, grip her under her arms, and slide her up until she straddles my hips. The tangy smell, the wet juices from her swiping across my skin threaten to drive me insane until I feel her warmth on my dick.

"Now, use that mouth on mine." Her wet lips hit mine with a rush. Yeah, I know my woman and that erogenous zone of a mouth of hers. There are many ways to turn my woman on; but you get inside her mouth, and she goes off in a matter of seconds.

She turns herself on without me even having to touch her when she's in a mood like this. She moans when I sweep my tongue across hers, tasting her like I can't get enough. This woman I'm desperately in love with is a magnet to my soul. I hold her face in my hands while I slip further into her mouth, sucking on her lips until I feel her toes curling under my ass. That's her habitual sign she's ready.

"You need to be fucked, Alina?" I ask her, knowing she does. She hasn't stopped rubbing her naked heat up against my straining dick since I brought her up here.

"That's a dumb question," she rasps out her response then bites my bottom lip while she slides one of my nipples in between her fingers and tugs.

"It sure is." I flip her over quickly, grab her ankles, shoving her legs in the air, and lean over the top of her. I grip my cock, placing him right where we both want him to be. Then I slam into her hard enough that the headboard hits the wall. She loves being fucked like this. Hard and deep. Her flexibility to arrange those long legs over my shoulders won't last much longer once she starts showing. Not that I mind. I can't wait to fuck her when her stomach is round and full.

Our bodies are slick with sweat as I continue to pound her tight body with an urgency to hit that deep, penetrating spot. Once I do, her head tilts back. Her wails of, "Right there, Roan" set my cock on fire to bring her where she needs to be, over the edge and into a state of sexual oblivion. To obtain the control of her body, to mark her for days so when I'm away from her for the next few days, she remembers me every time she moves.

"God, I love you so much," I tell her. Those eyes that shred me fly open. She looks at me as if I'm all she sees, all she wants in this fucked-up world we live in. I can't take my eyes off of her. She radiates both inner and outer beauty beyond any man's imagination. We're fucking wildly with our bodies while making love with our minds. I want to crawl into that love she has for me and never come out. I see her pain too. Pain that shoots from her heart to her eyes. She can't help but reveal it; it doesn't stop her from letting me hear those words that send me over the edge with her, to fill her deep with my release. To sate her with a love like no other.

"You come back to me and Alex, Roan."

Having no idea what time it is when I wake alone in bed, I can't help but crack what's possibly the only smile I'm going to have for God knows how long, and even though I'm grateful my brain shut down and my body feels rested, the minute I swing my legs over the bed, the usual assault of dread and worry that forces my smile to fade starts.

I slept through the entire evening. I have no idea if Calla called Cain, or what the fuck is going on with her. I know she's safe. If she weren't, I would have been told. After a good long stretch, I'm up and heading for the shower before joining everyone else to get started on the hundreds of things we have to do. I adjust the water to as hot as I can stand it, and although I could stay under it all day while the hammering spray beats the tension out of my neck and shoulders, I finish, quickly wrap a towel around my waist, finish the rest of my business, foregoing shaving once again, and bust my ass to get dressed, pack the clothes I need, and hit the hallway, only to run into both my mom and my aunt.

"Morning," my mom chippers out. Her mood seems to have improved; she even has on her Chanel perfume my dad bought her every year for Christmas. I can smell it lingering freshly in the air. That has to count for something. Maybe she's pushing her way back to the way she was before we pulled her happy mood from under her yesterday.

"Morning. You look good, mom. You too, Aunt Cecily," I tell them, then plant a kiss on each of their cheeks.

"Yeah, well, nothing will bring your dad back to us; then again, revenge is a beautiful thing. I have no choice but to live with that." Damn, she's wise and evil when she wants to be.

"I think I'll keep you around, old wise one." She laughs then draws me in for a hug.

"To answer your question, I'm leaving in a few hours. Need to settle some things with Cain, grab the other guys, then yeah, we're leaving." I kiss the top of her head after she lets me go. I keep my arm draped around her neck for comfort you can only get from your mother. I haven't told them where I'm going or why this early in the day, not when we really don't have to leave yet. There isn't much I can do until later this evening, but what I need to do now can't wait.

"We can say goodbye in a bit. You should eat since you missed both dinner and breakfast." She cocks her head, gives me that what-you-up-to-now look while twisting her body to pat the side of my face. My arm drops from around her, and another smile graces my face; that makes two, when I thought I'd only get one.

I have no clue what makes me want to get the hell out of this state and away from this life. Something does. I make a decision right there that when this is all over, I'm hopping on our jet with whomever the fuck wants to go and heading to Florida with my family like Alina suggested. I can work from there for a month or so. God, my dick twitches in my jeans from the thought of it. Get me the hell out of this fucking city, at least for a little while. I can almost feel the spray of the water hitting my face from the wall of rocks down the beach from our home. The sand all over the house, the boat rides with my son. Fuck, I'm all over it.

"What the hell time is it?" I ask informally as we descend the stairs. No more thinking about a vacation until that rotten scum is floating in the bottom of the ocean up here. I never glanced at the clock when I was rushing around getting ready.

"Eleven," Mom calls out.

"Son of a bitch. That late? Where're Alina and Alex?"

"Outside with everyone else. They're fine, Roan. Everyone is fine. Both you and Cain slept in; you needed it. Him especially." That comment stops me dead in my tracks at the bottom of the stairs. *I hope to God she means he decided to say 'the hell with it' and got drunk and passed out.* I know damn well he didn't. He may be a hotheaded son of a bitch, but he isn't irresponsible, not when it comes to his family's welfare.

"What the hell do you mean by that? And if something happened, don't you think someone should have woken me up?" Both women whip around and glare at me like I've lost my mind, which I have somewhere between my dad's death and the outcome of what's ahead.

"No. I took care of it. Besides, it's Cain, for god's sake. It won't matter what the hell happens between the moments Calla left here until the minute he sees her again. The man is going to worry."

"Look, Aunt Cecily. I have no doubt you handled it, but it's my right to know if something went down, even if it's as little as her stubbing her toe. I want to know. Could someone tell me, please?" Now I sound like my dad, begging and demanding at the same time.

"She handled it, all right, by not letting me talk to John when he called her." Cain walks around the corner looking like absolute shit.

"Wait, what? When did he call? I thought Calla was supposed to call. What the fuck?" I'm growing more agitated with each passing second. If they don't tell me what I need to know right the hell now, I'm going to blow up. I take a much-needed deep breath, drop my bag on the floor, and pinch the bridge of my nose, giving myself a moment to calm my raging nerves before I do exactly what I know will have everyone running in here freaking the fuck out. Like yell and beat on my chest, telling them to fucking tell me.

"You're reading more into this than necessary, Cain. Settle the hell down like I told you to. The two of you can discuss this in the office." Leave it to my aunt once again to save the fucking day by being reasonable, or should I say, night, because whatever has Cain in an uproar can't be good. Hence his reason for looking like he really did down an entire bottle of his Johnny Walker.

"I'll let Alina know you're up. Ask her to give you a few minutes, then you need to eat."

"Thanks, Mom," I calmly tell her before I follow this hardass of a brooding bitch into the office.

"What the fuck, brother?" I burst out after slamming the door behind us.

"Don't 'what the fuck' me. It isn't your wife out there risking her life on the arms of a bastard who had his hands planted all over her ass last night." I watch him pace the floor, his eyes wild in his manic head. That low blow was uncalled for, regardless if he's right or not in saying it. I would hate it so much I would lose my head over it. It would drive me to the brink of insanity. The only way to stop me from following her were if someone sedated me then strapped me down out in our electric chair and left me there. Something tells me that's really not the issue here though. It's something else that has him worked up to the point he's driving himself out of his mind.

"Wait. Last night? What are you saying? They were out in public last night? Well, fuck me, he really does move fast, doesn't he?" I almost burst out laughing, but the deadly look in his eyes stops me from doing so.

"Oh, yeah. They went out, all right. To some restaurant where Silas found out Donal was at."

"Man, you need to calm down. This is a good thing. It means our plan is already in motion."

"Fuck off." This time, I do laugh. I can't help it. Here I was thinking something bad happened like she was hurt or flipping out about doing this, when all it is, is Cain acting like a jealous husband over his wife acting. She must have done a damn good job for him to be rattled the way he is. Then it hits me like an eighteen-wheeler flattening me.

"How the hell did you know he had his hands on her ass?" He doesn't reply at first. He stands there staring blankly into space. I feel like I need to snap my fingers or some shit to get his attention. I don't. I wait for him to come to his senses, and when he does, he pulls his phone out of his pocket, fiddles around with it, and my eyes go wide at what I see.

"Shit." I snatch the phone from his hands and scroll and scroll through various photos plastered all over the place of her and Silas all over each other. "What in the ever loving fuck is she doing?" I seethe. He doesn't have to answer me. His pent-up frustration doesn't have a damn thing to do with her pretending. It has everything to do with the fact that every headline on these photos is calling her a traitor.

"Have you talked to her to make sure she's all right?" I ask him with a steady voice, then hand him his phone back. I don't want to see any more. I'm sure he doesn't either. There won't be a thing any of us can do to fix this. She's ruined.

"Yeah. I talked to her. She's fine. We all knew there was a chance it might happen. Doesn't mean it isn't bothering her or that this won't eat her up inside once this is over. She worked her ass off for that degree. I'm not mad at her or you. It's him. This is another thing he's stolen from us. From her." He's right. I go to tell him that everything will be fine, except it won't be fine, at least not for her. I settle on the truth. I've never lied to him before; I sure as hell am not going to now.

"Cain. Brother, she knew this would happen, man. You said so yourself. Instead of pissing yourself off even more, be proud of her. There aren't many people in this world who would sacrifice everything they have to bring someone else down. She gave that career up for her love for this family. For the love she has for you and Justice. I can't make it up to her, no matter what I do. The only thing I can and will do is promise you both that Calla will come out of this unscathed. Her career as a respected woman may be the talk of the town right now; that shit will die down as soon as those cockroaches find somewhere else to live." I lean up against the desk for support. It's not like all of us didn't talk about this briefly yesterday; we did. And now that the momentum of her career is the get-up-and-go topic of the underworld, I hope she's able to keep her head in this dangerous game.

"There's something you should know. Something John told Cecily last night." Cain grips the back of his neck with both hands, something he used to do all the time when the two of them were split up and he would get worked up whenever I reported something to him he didn't like. Fuck, he went as far as telling me never to look in her underwear drawer, because the woman had a fetish for the sexy little numbers. That pissed me off. I tossed the fact she was my blood in there and told him to go fuck himself, but to him, it didn't matter. All he thought about was that another man was seeing her, even if all those years I not once let her see me, nor spoke to her. The fucker needs a vacation worse than I do. He's causing my stress level to power through the roof.

"What did he say?" I ask reasonably instead of snapping like I want to. I need to be done here for selfish reasons of my own. I feel guilty for Calla losing the reputation she's worked hard to build. Overnight nonetheless, but we have to stay focused, have to ignore triggers that could set us off. We can't afford to lose our concentration, so whatever the hell he needs to tell me, he needs to make it quick. Every second I count under my breath is one less I can spend with my wife and son. My visit to the cemetery isn't going to happen as I hoped. I really wanted to talk to my dad before all this went down, but damn, the trip to the warehouse, where I can grab a particular knife that's been waiting for someone to come and use it, that cannot wait. That knife is going to be the weapon that takes Donal's life. The same one my brother carried around for years, the very one he sliced my finger off with. The only thing that was reliable to him until I got my hands on it. And now this fucker, who for whatever reason has shown up out of some kind of fucked-up loyalty to Royal, is going to die by it.

"Donal was at the restaurant last night. She talked to him."

"Come again? It sounded like you said she talked to Donal last night." This time, I do speak with defiance laced through my bitter voice.

"She did."

"And?" I force that one-syllable word out.

"It seems she has a new friend."

CALLA

"I'm really okay, Roan. I promise. Now, can we drop it and get to the reason why you're calling?" I've told this story three times already; this will make four. If I never have to talk about last night again, it won't be soon enough. Reliving it makes me feel like running to the bathroom and throwing up, then taking a cold shower to scrub my body raw from the filth I still feel coating my arms.

"Nothing happened," I lie. No one knows what he said to me except Silas when I disobeyed my dad's strict orders and Silas' demanding threats that I not go to the bathroom. I had to go; it was either throw up in public or in private. I chose to keep what little bit of dignity I could muster in a place where every person had their eyeballs rolling on the floor as they watched the two of us on public display.

At first, I thought their scrutiny and dirty looks that had my stomach tightening in fear was what brought the urge to vomit to the surface; then it was the cell phones the nosy high-classed bitches were so inconspicuously trying to hide; but that wasn't it at all. It was something else, something I didn't realize could be until this morning.

Of course, I felt sick again for completely different reasons than all of those combined when what he said to me caught me off guard after leaving the bathroom. How in the hell am I supposed to pull it off? There's no way in hell I can. And Silas, the man shocked the hell out of me when he threatened to tip off the cops about the fight if Donal didn't stay away from me. The man looked at Silas like he would kill him right there. Told him to go ahead and turn him in that he would be dead in his sleep tonight if I didn't do what he asked. He didn't back down from him; he just took ahold of me by my arm and discreetly walked us back to our table.

Who the hell is this guy and why, why in god's name does he think he holds all the power? He has met his match in me. I hold the goddamn power, not a man who thinks I will fuck him because he thinks I'm a whore. God, if Cain or my dad are to find this out, they will go on a manhunt and gut him without thinking twice about it. No. He has to suffer for what he has done. Pain needs to be upon him like he's never felt before. He will not get the easy way out when he dies.

We have to figure out the right way to go about this. To tell them the truth that Donal said the only way he'll believe I'm not a spy for my family is if I fuck him in between the first fight and Lorenzo's. It throws our plan off. Tilts it to his side until we can figure this out. I've let worry and fear snake through me, and it's a lethal combination I have to get out of my system before tomorrow night. He'll kill me if I don't, and he will dangle me in front of my entire family's face before he does so.

The words to tell Roan are right there on the tip of my tongue, to let him know I wanted to toss that dirty, sick, twisted fucker's words right back in his face. I don't and I won't. Not until the time is right.

I do know this though; if it weren't for Silas standing out there, waiting for me to come out, I would have shot the bastard right there. Thank God he followed me without me knowing it, or not only would I have ruined my career as I did, but I would also be hiring Deidre's dad to represent me for murder.

I love Roan, but I need this conversation to end. I can't talk about it anymore. My head is spinning with the need to expel all I know.

"He didn't come up to us until our drinks arrived. Before you ask, I only had one glass of wine." Even though my nerves were screaming at me to drink the entire bottle in one giant gulp, I knew I had to have my head clear to play this game. It was working until he showed up at our table. Then my nerves frayed into tiny little fragments. I kept them under control as best as I could on the outside. My insides, however, are destroyed.

"And Silas. How was he?" Roan asks with a hint of unease.

"He was a pro. The only thing I felt uncomfortable with him doing was placing his hand on my ass when we got up to leave. Other than that, he was a perfect gentleman. He kissed my hand, ran his fingers down my cheek. Come on, do you really need to know this part? I mean, it's right there on the Internet for you to see." He lets out a loud, disturbing moan in my ear. I shouldn't have said that. Now he'll think I'm not okay with the slander that's spread from here to Russia already about me. I'm sick of repeating myself about what happened between Silas and me. What Roan needs to know is Donal's reaction to seeing us together. He needs to know what he said about the fight and Lorenzo. Everything else is irrelevant at this point. It's water under the bridge as far as I'm concerned. Well, the meaningless chitchat is. The part about me fucking him after the first fight is over is most definitely not.

I catch him before he can say anything more about my career when I hear him sigh through the phone again. He feels guilty. I'm tired of guilt, shame, and all that goes with it. Completely over it. All I want to do is crawl into bed and sleep. After last night, then lunch with Lorenzo and Sandman, and on top of the news I'm positive about, I'm exhausted.

"Listen, let me tell you about Donal, then I'm going to bed. I suggest you do the same. Tomorrow will be here before we know it," I say, then carry right into what needs to be said.

"I felt his eyes on me the minute we stepped onto the curb. I played my role; Silas played his. We gave him a show. We sat there and talked about Lorenzo. At times, we would lean over the table, pretending to whisper quietly; then others, we made sure we were loud enough for him to hear. Lucky for me, he had no clue I knew who he was. I played dumb whenever I would glance over his way. Gave him a polite smile, then turned my attention right back to Silas." I pause to catch my breath and swallow the nausea that's ready to spew out of my mouth from restating these words once again. I leave out the parts about every time I leaned over the table I made sure to show enough cleavage. I wanted him to notice me. I just didn't expect him to proposition me a half hour after I met the prick.

"At first, when he walked up to us, I ignored him, took a sip of my wine, and stared out the window as the two of them chatted about the fight. He was polite when Silas introduced us, Roan, a perfect gentleman. The only out of line thing he said was he was shocked to see the two of us together," I lie. Christ, I hate doing this. If I tell him or anyone, they will pull this plan, call it off, and bring me home. I refuse to let that happen.

"That's good then. Our plan is working." He speaks with ease this time though I can still hear the apprehension in his voice. I suppose I would feel the same way if the tables were turned and it were him.

"Right, it is. Anyway, after he spoke those words, I answered him just like we planned. I told him Silas came to me for direction on an out-of-state case. We immediately felt drawn to each other, then after several months, we got tired of hiding it, so I left my family. I shrugged like it was no big deal in hopes to throw off any warning or suspicions. I'm sure he's tried to check into it. We all know he won't find any reason not to believe me, but then again, who knows what he'll do with this information. I mean, he'd be as dumb as a rock if he weren't checking us out. He seems to know our move before we do anyway."

"Stop right there," he bellows out, causing me to pull the phone from my ear in confusion. Now, what did I say that has him all bent out of shape? It's my turn to sigh and moan.

"You better be worried. I sure as hell am. Fuck, Calla." I sit up in bed when I feel as if he's going to pull me off of doing this.

"Roan, I'm not backing out. Silas is not backing out. That man cannot possibly suspect what we have planned; there is no way. Don't doubt me on this. I'm not worried if he is, Roan, not with Dad here and definitely not with you guys surrounding the place tomorrow night." My pulse starts to beat loudly in my ears. My blood pressure is rising.

"There's no way we can back out. The contact has been made. All they need to do now is wait. It's... fuck, Calla. Do you understand how hard it is for me to allow you to do this? It should be me, not you." I can barely hear him through the agony pilfering through his voice. It irritates and soothes me at the same time. I take a deep breath, and as much as I love my cousin, I ignore his grounds he's trying to express. He's scared. I'm scared. We're all scared. I can't be that cruel to him though, can I? The air needs to be clear between us. The same as when I spoke to Cain this morning; well, more like he yelled and I listened. I don't think I'll forget the pain crackling in his voice. "I've loved you since we were sixteen years old, Calla. Those years we were apart, I lived in hell. I'm worried out of my mind about you. Fuck, babe, this is so damn wrong." He finally caught his breath long enough for me to tell him to go to the bathroom and strip naked. The release we gave ourselves while talking dirty to each other was enough to ease his tension down a couple of degrees. All it did for me was make me feel guilty. Right here and now isn't about me; it's about my cousin. He deserves peace.

"Well, you can't be here, and we all know it. I'm the only choice, the best choice. Trust and family, remember?" I grin, only for the reason that he chuckled for some odd reason.

"Then," I say evenly with a huge, exaggerated extension of the word, "he asked if I was coming to the fight. I told him I wouldn't miss it for anything. That Silas loved these fights, and it was a pleasure to finally meet the man who gave my guy something he enjoyed besides me and work. He left our table, went back to his date, and that was it. We ate and left." For years, I've lied every day in a courtroom to defend my clients, and now that I'm lying to protect those I truly love, it makes me want to spit out the truth. A lie is a lie, no matter if it's to cover your ass or someone else's. This is why I've memorized every word I've said over and over in my head so much that the anxiety is increasing for fear I will say the wrong thing and get caught. However, when I tell these lies to every man in my life I love, it goes against everything I deem to be right.

"You did well, Calla. As long as you're positive you're all right, then I'll check in with you tomorrow afternoon before you leave." The pit of my stomach falls when he says tomorrow. Whatever happens, tomorrow is going to be the end. If ever I needed God on my side of the dark, it would be tomorrow.

"Be safe, Roan," I say into the silent phone.

I lie in bed for several long minutes after we hang up, that guilt and shame clawing at my throat, scraping it raw. I have no idea how I got through today with lying to my dad about any of it; well, I do. Because now, he's worried sick about me. Lying to someone's face is harder than lying over the phone, so what did I do? I lied some more. As far as he knows, I've been suffering from the oldest excuse in the book: a tension headache. One so bad that it's caused me to wake this morning only to throw up, to eat lunch only to throw up, and now, as my stomach crashes from the panic assailing my entire nervous system, I feel like throwing up again. All of it is a lie, because as I lie here knowing I have to get up and walk across the hall to give Dad back his phone, I identify the signs. I'm pregnant.

I roll over onto my side as I feel the tears fall down my face onto my pillow. Dad wasn't in his room when I went to give him his phone. I left it on his bed, shut the door to the bedroom I'm sleeping in, and crawled right back into bed.

I don't know what to do. I made Silas promise me not to go back and tell anyone what that animal said he wanted from me. He hasn't betrayed my trust yet; if he did, my dad would barrel down this door and drag me out of here.

"Dad." I jump when the door opens to reveal the light pouring in from the hallway.

"Hey, sweetheart. Wanted to check to see if you were all right before I checked in with your mom and Roan. I brought you some toast and coffee." My chest begins to hurt from the kindness he's showing me. The worry I'm sure is gnawing at him.

"What time is it?" I sit up and yawn.

"It's eight." He lightly laughs then sets the plate and cup on the nightstand. I must have fallen right to sleep after taking his phone to his room.

"You should eat this." He points to the food, then sits on the side of the bed, studying my features intently.

"I will, dad. I'm sorry about yesterday and last night. I think my nerves are getting the best of me," I lie. I do it so well, I can't tell if he believes me or not when he reaches over, picks up the plate of toast, and hands it to me.

"Eat that. It's cinnamon and butter." He says again. The smell makes me nauseous. I want to throw up and dry heave. My muscles are cramping from my toes to my stomach from holding it in.

"It smells good," I say and take a bite, internally gagging as I chew and swallow.

"Great. I'm going to go work out. You should get up and shower. The stylist will be here in a few hours to do all that fancy shit to you," he says with a slight smile.

"How fun." I roll my eyes then reach for the coffee.

"Let me call them; then I'll give you the phone to call Cain." He pats my leg and kisses my forehead with apprehension like he did when I was a little girl. Even the kind gesture of him bringing my favorite toast has me wanting to tell him to take me home, to tell him I'm scared, this is all a mistake, but I'm too weak of a woman to do it.

"And Calla," he says my name confidently.

"I'm not sure why you won't tell me what's really bothering you; whatever it is, I want you to know I have faith in you." With parting words that rip through the aura of mixed colors in my soul, he turns and leaves, taking the lump in my throat with him. The floodgates open, leaving me no choice but to cry.

"You look stunning, Calla." Silas looks me over when I reach the top of the stairs. I'm wearing a gold crop top embellished with tiny multi-colored sparkles, a pair of skin-tight, black leather pants, and five-inch matching sparkling Jimmy Choo's. I had no idea what to wear when I packed in a flurry. I brought designer jeans and a red tank top. However, the pleasant surprise on his face tells me my surprise stylist he sent over did his job.

I managed to eat my toast and drink my coffee without throwing up, which is a good thing. Even though, when I called Cain, I was hardly able to keep my wits about the fear that something terribly wrong is going to happen; it almost had me breaking down when, much to my surprise, my own stylist Mateo Delacroix was the one Silas hired to make me over for tonight. "Get over here and give me some love," he demanded. I went willingly. "You didn't bring color with you by chance?" I jokingly said when we made our way down to my room. His boisterous laughter at my comment was just what I needed. "Girl, you wouldn't make it to wherever you're going with all that hair you have going on if I colored it. Besides, that mighty fine man of yours would kick my ass if I colored this hair." He's been doing my hair for years. A handful of times, he's fancied me up with a designer dress, hair, and makeup for charity functions. Never like this though, and never where it's only been the two of us where I was able to break down and let out my darkest fears. I took it as an answer from above, to be able to tell someone who's heard stories that would blow someone's mind I was a hundred percent sure I was pregnant, which had him squealing in delight until I told him no one knew.

He didn't pry about why my dad and I were here. Although he knows exactly who I am and what my family does. Almost everyone in this city and beyond knows who we are. Famous in our own right as a mafia family, who lives off of thievery. He also knows Silas, therefore, when I finally told him it was business why we were here, he knew not to ask. However, as he was applying my dark, sultry makeup on my eyes, he let me know he's heard the rumors and didn't believe a single one of them. He made me feel brave, beautiful, and bold to stand here and carry this through without even comprehending he was doing so.

My Dad left a few hours ago. Told me it was unsafe for him to ride over to the fight with us. He disappeared like the wind, leaving me alone. I guess Silas has proven his loyalty for him to walk out and leave me. But I know the minute I step out of the vehicle, he will never take his eyes off of me. How he's gone about getting himself inside without being seen beats the shit out of me. The man has lived most of his adult life roaming around like a panther, never once getting caught.

"Thank you. You really didn't have to do this," I tell him yet again. He insisted on it yesterday. Said that even though there are blood and men beating the hell out of each other, that every woman in there dresses to the highest degree.

"You must have paid a pretty penny for Mateo. How did you know he was my stylist?" I question, lifting my eyes to meet his.

"Your mother." He shrugs.

"This was her doing?" I ask, all of it making sense now.

"Yes and no. I told her I wanted to do something nice for you, to make you comfortable, because I know what it's like for you to sacrifice yourself for someone you love. She told me she knew exactly what she thought would make you feel good. She handled getting him here. As far as the money goes, he wouldn't take a dime, Calla."

"Oh," I flutter out. I desperately want to ask him what he means about sacrificing. The way he stares back at me with pleading eyes not to pry makes me take a few steps forward and catch him by surprise as I place a kiss on his cheek.

"You really do look stunning. It's such a waste of beauty for you to be on my arm instead of your husband's tonight. Is he okay?" he asks.

Lunch yesterday was staged perfectly to impress the shocked reactions were the rumors. A kiss here, a loving touch there. For a brief moment it had me forgetting all about missing Cain and Justice. I feel like I can't breathe without them. Knowing I'm sacrificing for them, for everyone has me going out of my mind with worry on how this could affect them if something goes wrong. My daughter growing up without me, my husband lost in this world. It's all too much and yet I know I've made the right choice.

We couldn't talk about anything else, not with Sandman and my dad in the vehicle. Nor with Lorenzo or Sandman sitting with us during lunch. I did find out more about Sandman and all he's been through. It angers me to think that he's been going through hell for years and now he's willing to sacrifice his life too. So him asking about Cain is not only a nice gesture, it's the first time we've been able to talk freely.

"He will be. I'm tired of my family being victims to people with a jealous rage. It's a loss I'll take over and over again to save them from any more pain," I say truthfully.

"And what about you, Calla. Are you going to be fine too? I mean, I'm not one to sit around and listen to gossip all day. However," he says with a lifted brow.

"Yeah, well, the however is none of anyone's business. There's nothing to be done about it. It's not like I can organize a press conference and say, 'Hey, the rumors were all a lie. We did what we had to do to kill someone.' I have to let it go. I don't owe them an explanation for my actions. As far as my career goes, I didn't give it up for this; I gave it up for my family. That I can live with."

"Well, they're lucky to have you. So are the rest of us. I don't think you understand that not only have you given up something you love for your family but for all the rest of us too. This man is a monster in his own screwed up head, a man who doesn't play by the rules. He's a threat to us all, Calla. Now, I'm not the sentimental type, so let's get this show on the road. Sandman should be here any minute. I have our plan figured out. But first, I need to know how you that you trust me. You're basically putting your life in my hands. "

"I'm frightened," I admit. "However, for a man who is willing to sacrifice his own life, to walk into someone else's territory knowing what we know about this immoral man, I trust you."

"You ready for this?" Both Sandman and Silas ask at the same time when we pull into the lot of an old brick warehouse. The parking lot is packed already. The first fight doesn't start for an hour. However, with the weekend traffic, it took us two hours to get here, and now with us pulling up to our reserved parking spot and Silas taking his phone out of his pocket to make the call to Roan, I'm scared of my mind. My family is going to kill me if I'm not slaughtered in here first.

"Yes," I say in a shaky breath. "Make the call."

"Goddamn it, Calla." The loud roar of Roan's voice echoes through the speaker on the phone after Silas and I explain the necessary change of plan and the reason behind it to Roan.

"It's the only way, Roan. If I had told you last night, you would have called this whole thing off." A shudder ripples through me when I'm met with silence for several drawn-out seconds before he calmly speaks again.

"I would have. I still should. It's a damn good thing everyone is already in place. Don't think for one minute I'm not going to choke the shit out of you the first chance I get. Silas, do not let go of her hand. Not for a motherfucking second."

My quivering lips turn up into a half smile from his outburst. He's pissed, and I understand why. It will make Donal's death that much more of a revenge for him to gladly rid him from his miserable life. The only thing that has changed is the time when Silas is to send the text to Roan. Other than that, we exit the vehicle and enter the loud warehouse as planned.

People are everywhere, drinking, laughing, and placing their bets. Some of the men acknowledge Silas with a pat on the back or a cordial hello as we walk back. All of them believe Lorenzo is his guy, that he's the one the people I overhear rumor to be the next champion. I'm shaking as I take in my surroundings. I've never seen anything like this in my life. I feel like I'm inside of a famous arena. There's a closed-in cage in the middle of the room. On one side, men are sitting at a table with computers in front of them, tapping away like there's no tomorrow. Rows of chairs surround the rest of the floor. Some women dressed as provocatively as they could get away with, while others are dressed simple yet classy.

"Here we are, babe." Silas hasn't let go of my hand the entire walk around the large room. He raps hard on the door of the dressing room he informed me we would go to first. Lorenzo ushers us inside, and still in the confines of this room, Silas doesn't let go of my hand. I have no idea why until Lorenzo greets me with a hug and whispers the word 'cameras' in my ear. All I can do is hug him back with my free arm, keep my panic inside, and act normal, not like I'm certifiably going out of my mind.

I'm fine as I stand there and watch Sandman and a few other men move around the room, talking and taping up Lorenzo's hands, lightly smacking him on his head, giving him a pep talk of verbiage that's as foreign to me as the slang you hear on the streets.

"You kick his ass," Silas demands before we walk out the door and head to our seats. All of this is happening so fast my head starts reeling, while my stomach is tossing. This is it. It's show time.

"You okay?" Silas pretends like he's leaning in for a kiss. Instead, he takes hold of both of my hands, allowing them to dangle in between us while he places his forehead up against mine.

"She will be. Change of plans." Both of our heads turn at the same time to the sound of a thick, heavily Irish accent.

Again, everything happens fast at the same time it reels out like an early slow motion movie.

The lights go out. Complete darkness surrounds me. All I hear is screaming and yelling, shuffling of feet. I stay where I am, holding on to Silas, gripping his hand as the fear is pumping through my veins. Then I'm pulled to the side right before I hear a gun going off, the rigorous boom causing my ears to pop.

That's when the darkness around me turns to pitch black and Silas' hand slips away from mine.

ROAN

"Change of plans. Get her out of there now!" I bark out my order to Rodney Stauffer the cop my dad trusted on the phone. "Let's go," I say anxiously to Dilan and Aidan after hanging up and making sure my phone is on vibrate then shoving it in my front pocket. "I can't believe she did this," I thunder out loud enough that if my voice were exactly a loud boom, it would be followed by a conniving white light that scattered across the inky black sky. I want to choke her for this. Yell at her until her bones shake and hug her at the same damn time. Jesus, what the hell is she thinking?

"She's fine, man. John will call you the second he has her. Keep your cool, grab that fucker, and we're out of here. No sticking around waiting; we'll all be fucked it we do. You got me, Roan?" Dilan has been giving me a talk since I hung up the phone with Calla and Silas a little over an hour ago. I'm not sure what in the hell she thinks she has to prove here, but her damn life is a lot more important than this revenge. I'm going to strangle her.

"Roan, did you fucking here me? You need to keep your head where it belongs. Now, slow the fuck down." I stop just outside of the entrance to the abandoned warehouse to catch my breath. My body is running on a full tank to get there, while my head is operating on fumes. My heart is racing, and it doesn't have a damn thing to do with the fact I'm practically sprinting to get to the side of the building, where Rodney reported he saw the little Irish prick park his royal blue Ferrari and enter through a side door. Royal fucking blue? Seriously. That's taking it a little too damn far. Goddamn joke is what it is.

"I want him bad, but not at the expense of anything happening to her," I say, then lean over with my hands on my knees to suck in some needed air. I'm shaking. I'm scared. And if I don't get that phone call from my uncle by the time I have that son of a bitch in my hands, I may go feral on him right there.

"We got to go. There's no time to stand here," Aidan pronounces. "Come on, brother; she's going to be okay. I know it." He places his big hand on my shoulder, his big, burly way to comfort me. All I can do is hope like a motherfucker he's right. If she isn't, I don't know what the hell I will do. Live the rest of my days in the dark with no way out, that's what.

"I hope you're right," I say, sending up a prayer that for the sake of every member of my family it's true.

"We're in place." Dilan's words to Rodney slice through the humid air once we reach our destination. It was easy to scale through the packed parking lot, weaving behind cars, always on the lookout for that stray who was left behind. He's now perched on the other side of Donal's car, while Aidan and I are standing on either side of the door. At the moment, there isn't a person in sight. Either they're inside, ready to get the shit rattled out of them, necks snapped in half, then dragged into the woods, or they're already headed to who knows where in the back of a police cruiser. Shit happened real fast the minute I hung up with her and called my contact. I sat in the car with Dilan, Aidan, and Lenny, watching the entire scene unfold. I swear to God it was like watching Ninjas sweep in out of nowhere and take these guards down.

Rodney said he'd handle it; so far he's pulled through. S.W.A.T. team and all. Now, if they'll stay the hell away from us, we can hopefully catch this fucker and be out of here before anyone realizes we had a thing to do with it.

The now empty front of this parking lot will be flooded with people in less than two minutes if this raid goes according to plan. Hopefully, Rodney can distract them from back here for at least a few minutes longer so we can get the hell out of here. I take a deep breath and stare at the black SUV where Ivan and Anton are perched waiting for the parking lot lights to go out like the rest of us. I know there isn't a chance in hell we're going to pull this off without some major flaw. I just need to remain optimistic it doesn't have a thing to do with her safety.

"Remember, Lorenzo said he made sure this door was locked from the inside. No one else has been seen going in this way but him," Dilan reminds me once again. I'm silently thanking a city official for delivering me the plans to this building. I had no idea if the scum would use this door or walk in the front. Knew my intuition paid off when I received the text from Lorenzo letting me know he had arrived and sure as shit came in this door. Pansy ass motherfucker.

I jump when the darkness hits us out of nowhere. I start to count rapidly in my head, knowing that any moment, people are going to be screaming their heads off, trying to claw their way through the dark. My heart is pounding its way out of my chest now, my eyes automatically searching around, trying to adjust to the blackness. This has to work. Christ, it has to. We're trying to pull off the oldest trick in the book: a goddamn police raid. It was the only option we had to try and make sure this shit got shut down. The cops, detectives, and the fucking FBI won't suspect a thing when the leader of this organization can never be found. They'll think he fled the country. At least that's the plan. Hell, Rodney's going to come out of this a goddamn hero when this shit is all over. He got a tip tonight that there was some illegal fighting and gambling happening here. Little do they know he received that tip a few days back when I trusted my dad that Rodney was loyal. The whole thing was planned out before the caller made the anonymous tip several hours ago, and Calla about fucked it all up. God, I'm pissed at her.

"Here come the screams. Watch for him. You know he doesn't give one fuck about anyone else. His ass will be out here," Dilan hollers from behind the car, causing me to snap my head in the direction of the screams.

"I would be too if all of a sudden the lights go out and the people start screaming 'cops' or 'raid.'" I nearly choke on Aidan's perception of how this shit is going down like a movie, yet once again, it's the first time I actually feel optimistic that we can pull this off. That I can finally get my hands on this self-righteous sociopath.

When the door swings open, I know it's him when no one rushes out. The rush, the adrenaline, the high-pitched screams filtering through the open doorway echo as they all worry about getting themselves to safety.

Seconds tick by and still nothing. I'm scaled up against the wall on this side of the wide open door. He knows we're out here.

My phone remains silent, my nerves are prickling, and I'm ready to fucking blow.

I draw my gun, ready to call him out to meet his fate when my phone vibrates in my pocket. Keeping my eyes wide open, I silently thank God my uncle has her, except there isn't a way for me to check. One move, one deep breath, and he'll know right where I am. It continues to vibrate against my leg, sending off a terrifying pulse so intense I feel paralyzed. Uncle John wouldn't fire off one right after the other; he's right to the point, which means either he can't find her or... I'm not waiting to get that answer. I can't.

"Where is she, motherfucker?" My voice is roaring over the loud sirens as they draw closer. Tons of them are coming from every direction. This fucker better hurry up, or he's going to prison, where I'll gladly find someone to broomstick his goddamn ass.

"Hopefully lying on the floor, bleeding to death while being trampled on, you fucking scum-sucking pig." Fear hits my spine as images of Calla on the floor and blood everywhere while people run her over like she means nothing to them hit me.

Out of every picture I've foreseen in my mind on how this would play out, her being abused by passerby who don't have the decency to pick her up and run was not one of them. It fuels my anger toward him more.

All rationality inside of me is evicted. I turn into an unrecognizable man to myself. My target is in between me and a door. I swing my body in front of that door, gun drawn to the quick. If he pops me, then he does. His eyes go wide when he sees me standing there in the vague light that's streaming out from the hallway where he stands.

"You and me, bitch," I say with an ejected release of the ice water flowing through my veins. I've been waiting for this high, to have it sliding through my body, its toxic substance consuming my thoughts, my intentions, and my life.

"I'll kill him," Donal punctures out, his accent thick, a knife resting at the perfect angle to slice Silas' throat.

"We're playing that game, are we now, Donal? Come on, man. Surely, a professional like you can do better than that. You know as well as I do that I don't give a fuck if you kill him. A pawn holds no value, dude. Not when you're King," I shrug. "He means jack to me. The minute you kill him is the minute you're mine anyway, so do it. In fact, I dare you. Slice his goddamn throat." I'm not about to look at Silas. I see the knife. Silas doesn't expect me to say a word either. He knows the drill. There is no way I will negotiate. No way will I take my eyes away from my prize. His word means shit when I can see the blood from my sharp vision sifting out of Silas' side, a blotch of blood staining through his white dress shirt. Either this fucktard is lying about Calla or he shot them both. Either way, I'm not taking a chance of letting him get away.

"He's a goddamn liar. The bullet grazed me. She's long gone with everyone just as planned…"

Doanl starts to slice his throat. That's when it hits me that I'm tired of waiting for the universe to deal me a good hand. Therefore, at this moment, the only thing I hear is the constant thump of my heart, the rush of finally having this spineless puppet in my line of sight giving me an itchy trigger finger. I aim my gun, I fire, and I nail him in the shoulder, causing him to drop the knife. Before he has a chance to reach for it, I've cleared Silas out of the way, and my hands are gripping his throat.

"Let's take this game somewhere else, shall we?" My fingers dig into his neck as I begin to cut off his air supply. On impulse, he fights with all he has. It's no good when Dilan slams the butt of his gun up against his skull, causing his eyes to roll to the back of his head. Still, he stands, eyes crazed, knowing he's going to die but not backing down.

"Get him the fuck out of here." I release my grip and make a mad dash for the SUV while pulling my phone out of my pocket. It's not going to do me a bit of good to check the text; nothing will until I hear her voice.

"Go," I tell Anton before I have the door shut, blocking out Silas' moaning while saying something about Calla. I place the phone to my ear, and a sigh of relief spans throughout me when she answers.

"Calla, are you okay?" Worry is snaking through my voice.

"Yes. Are all of you? Silas, I… I think he was shot." She's uncertain and full of alarm. I look over to Dilan hovering over Silas, who's mumbling out how he wants to fry Donal's balls, while Dilan assesses his wound. Then slowly, I look behind me to a calm Aidan, who has Donal already gagged and put zip ties around his hands and feet.

Renewed energy fills my chest to the brim. "He's going to be fine. We're all going to be fine."

"Yeah, we are."

~

"I feel a resurrection coming. Long live the King," I say, elatedly. I don't have a goddamn clue where we are. All I know is, Ivan is guiding us toward a boat I've never seen before. When you plan a raid with your cousin volunteering to be the bait all within a couple of hours, you tend to leave a few of the formalities to someone you trust. Like where to kill and dump the body. It's ironic that the last time I was on a boat was when I came close to killing my brother. It's fitting that his fuckbuddy is about to meet his demise on a boat as well.

"The boat is set. Let's go," Ivan instructs. We've been driving in the direction of my parents' home for about a half hour. The first ten minutes or so, I talked to Calla and my uncle in one ear while listening to Aidan get his shit kicks in on Donal before we dropped him off at one of our warehouses where he left his truck. We need it to drive back home.

"Who's driving this thing?" I ask, then drag a quiet captive by the man bun on the back of his head, his body hitting face first onto the cement.

"He isn't going to talk; you know that, right?" Dilan starts to drag him by his hair. Goddamn, that has to sting.

"Doesn't matter. He'll hear everything I have to say before he dies. He can squat in a fucking corner with my brother and pray to a god who won't listen to either one of them. I know why he did it; there isn't a thing he needs to say except 'Forgive me, Father, for I have sinned.' You'll be repeating that in hell, you fucking wanker." We both ignore my joke when I hear Ivan say.

"Cain is."

"Cain is what?" I enquire, confused.

"Driving the boat." He points to where Cain is standing at the back of the fishing boat, hands on his hips, and smile on his face.

"Well, fuck," I say, all the while wondering if he had the opportunity to see Calla before he got here.

"Have you seen her?" It's the first thing I ask after climbing on board behind Dilan and Aidan, who have our quiet yet untamed prisoner sprawled out across the back of the boat and are beginning to secure his legs to the chain on the anchor. I guess now is the time he thinks he should try and resist. Good thing there's tape over his mouth. I'd hate to have to cut his tongue out before I have the chance to at least offer him any final words.

"Yeah, for a few minutes. Besides being shaken up and a nice hand-printed bruise on her arm she's good."

"And my mom?" I ask.

"She's fine, man. Anxious to see you, to know it's finally over." He watches me intently, that cocky tip of his lip smile hitting me in the chest. All four of us are here. We've been through the troubles each one of us has had. Our women being kidnapped, threats most of our lives. None of us are indestructible, but given the tight bond we have with each other, there isn't a single one who could be replaceable.

"Thanks for staying back with them. I know it wasn't easy. You're here now though, right where you should be."

"Wouldn't want to be anywhere else, except in bed with my wife. I know damn well that's where you want to be too. Let's do this. Let's kill the fucker," he says with a pat on my back and a solid kick to Donal's face, making him grunt as he tries to mumble angrily under the tape. His savaged eyes show no fear whatsoever; only the same desire to kill stares back at me as the blood from his nose trails down his face, hitting the tarp underneath him.

"You gentlemen have a nice fishing trip," Anton calls out.

"Not going?" I turn to train my attention on them.

"Nah. This is all you. Besides, you haven't been seen for days. As far as anyone knows, the four of you borrowed Alexei's old boat I kept after he died. This is your kill, brother. Just make sure one of those limbs you rip off is in the name of Alexei and we're good."

"My pleasure. Thank you." I lean in to shake both of their hands.

"You did well, Roan. Now finish this, get back to my girl, and get the hell out of here for a while. We'll talk, my son, soon." Instead of feeling like less of a man for the tears that spring free of my eyes at his sentiment, I feel more like one, knowing the meaning behind his words. He's telling me I'm only one meaningful death away from avenging a death that never should have happened.

I hear Cain cut the engine about an hour after sitting in the nearly pitch dark, twirling the knife that belonged to my brother in my hand the entire time. I haven't taken my eyes off the face of the man who has taken so much from me. I wanted to kill him slowly, to watch the many phases of his facial expressions as I cut off every limb of his body. Now that we've stopped, all I want to do is take this jagged-edged knife and start with his head, so I never have to look at his face again.

"Come on, man, let's get this done. Just like you, we all want this over." Cain rests his hand on my shoulder. Aidan and Dilan are standing on my other side. The boat begins to rock back and forth without the heavy anchor and chain to slow its drag.

I toss that all overboard. In a matter of minutes, this piece of shit will be following, and like my mom said, she never wants to speak of him again. Neither do I.

I lean forward on my haunches, my face inches from his, desperation clawing at me to let him speak. There's not a chance in hell I want to hear anything he has to say.

"I've never wanted to kill anyone as much as I do you. Not even Royal. Trust me; I wanted to kill him in the worst way. But you, you killed my father. Then you couldn't stop there, could you? You went and took the lives of two innocent people, and for what? To prove that you could. No one takes away from me and lives. The short life you lived must have been hell for you, motherfucker, to have hatred rooted so deeply inside of you that you plot some sick, twisted scheme to knock off your own dad. I'm not a biblical man; something tells me you're not either. I can only imagine what hell is like. It has to be a furnace down there, pits of flames and darkness. I wonder if the devil judges his people by the crimes he commits here; the worse the sin, the more punishment you receive. Can you imagine eternally quenching in a burning wind of fire, one that has you weeping, gnashing your teeth because the pain never goes away? You're tormented forever." He can't answer me; all he does is stare back with an expression of pure pleasure on his face. He's not afraid to die; he knows I will forever live in my own personal hell on earth. That I will never forget what he took from me. I won't. Knowing that I took his life is the only thing that will give me enough peace to make it through the dark hours even in the light of day.

"Give me five minutes then drop the anchor," I say with malice dripping from my voice.

"Hold him down by his shoulders," I request.

"You can rot in hell knowing one thing. You'll be my favorite kill, Donal. My absolute favorite." With those parting words and the serrated blade of the knife that was used on my wife, on Calla, and me, I start with one finger at a time, tossing each one overboard, drowning out his screams through the tape covering his mouth. Every digit I take off feels better than the last.

"Tell my brother this is my empire." Fire blazes from my mouth, but it does nothing to melt the hard, icy stare I give him. A meaty popping sound fills the air as I cut through every corded vein straining in his neck, the blood squirting all over the three of us as it drains away from his brain, its warmth penetrating through the gloves I put on. The gurgling noises that stem from his throat to his nose sound like he's trying to breathe through a thin paper bag. My muscles strain when I reach the cord on his spine, his almost lifeless body kicking and twitching against the restraints. I stop, knowing I want the blood to ooze out of him while we drag his body around the ocean to attack the sharks. I won't dock this boat until I know every piece of his flesh has been eaten off of him.

"Roll him up."

EPILOGUE

CALLA

One month later.

It's not every day a woman can sit on the beach and watch her husband jump the waves with their daughter. Her joyous laughter is ringing out above the crashing of those waves.

Our relaxing month at our vacation home in the Florida Keys has come to an end. Justice starts kindergarten in a week. That in itself is hard to believe. I'd give anything to turn time back to the day she was born, yet keep her the same age as she is now. She will always be our baby.

Now though, as I sit here with my knees propped up, my body laced with nothing but ease, I have another baby to soon make memories with. I sigh as I watch the two of them playing, her hair a salty mess, both of their skins a golden brown. Things could have gone differently a month ago. I could have lost another baby.

I contemplated not telling him that I suspected I was pregnant before I entered that warehouse. I couldn't do it. We'd promised one another no more secrets or lies. He went off on a wild tangent of how irresponsible I was to tempt fate as I did. I let him say what he needed to say, only to toss in one rebuttal.

"How can you tempt fate when fate tempts you?" I'm not sure what went through his head at that moment; whatever did softened him up to have him lean me back on the bed and devour me with soft kisses to my stomach while murmuring for me to promise him never to volunteer to put my life in danger again.

"I promise," I had said, easily.

If I never have to go through another mind fucking for the rest of my life, it won't be too soon.

I gained more trust from the other families, who suspected it was us behind that bust, than I earned. None of that matters when I lost more.

I gave up my career to stand where my uncle wanted me to be. It was my choice to do so. To stand around and watch your name be raked through the murky waters, because that's how shallow people are when gossip arises. They talk, they spread rumors, and they thrive on making someone else's life a living hell. I thought it would bother me. Instead, it did the opposite. I'm not saying I won't miss doing what I loved to do. I will miss it for the rest of my life. But it doesn't compare to missing out on the scene before me or to watch my stomach grow with another life Cain and I created. That's something that can never be taken away from us. Everything else in life runs far behind the love we have for one another.

I smile and regain my thoughts to the here and now when I see the rest of the family strolling down the beach. Aidan is looking like a big giant teddy bear carrying him and Deidre's three-week-old son, Dray, in a cloth baby carrier draped around his neck and shoulders. His big hands support the tiny bundle. I stand and place my hand over my tiny bundle growing inside of me that isn't more than a size of a peanut while

I wait for them to reach me. Roan dashes to the water behind Alex.

My gaze stays trained on them, watching him scoop his son up and on top of his shoulders then running into the waves with Dilan and him and Anna's son hot on their tails. It's a beautiful sight to see.

Roan and I shoved the work behind us the whole time we've been down here. There is nothing more important than this waiting for us back there. Nobody's home. Everyone hopped on a private chartered plane to come down here. The only ones not here are Alina's parents, her brothers, and their families. Someone had to stay behind to keep a close eye on things. There isn't anyone more trustworthy than him, well, besides Silas. He proved how trusting he could be by saving my life when we all know that bullet was meant for me. He shoved me out of the way. That's why I felt his hand slip from mine. A man who I thought wouldn't give up his life for another the day I met him proved me wrong. He was willing to give it up for me. How can you not trust someone who would do such a thing?

He's here now. Heading toward me with a shit eating grin on his face after doing some damage control with his own business back home. He still has a small, puckered scar across the side of his stomach where the bullet took a small chunk of his skin.

"You good?" he asks. It's the same question he asks me every day. One I should be tired of but won't ever be.

"Yeah, and you?"

"Yeah. It's been great down here. Relaxing in a way I can't describe. I'm ready to get back home though. Can't put off our lives forever, you know?"

"I do know," I say with trepidation. My new life as a woman once admired and now scorned will soon take rein over my days. I'm prepared. After all, with Roan and me, blood truly is thicker than water. It's a vibrant whir of swirling emotions. Kill after the kill. Blood after the blood. That's what he did the night he put our years of one nightmare after the other for us to rest peacefully, and for the man whose name is forbidden to come out of any of our mouths again, per my aunt's request, to live eternally in one nightmarish hell after the other. He killed him. No more pain can be cast upon my family from Royal's desire ever again. The last of his revenge rots somewhere in the bottom of the ocean.

"She's glowing already," my mom says, her sing-song voice joyfully praising. That woman is a walking contradiction of sugary compliments lately. I train my attention on her and my aunt. My beautiful aunt, who looks healthier than I've seen her since this horrendous loss of ours happened.

"I'm barely two months," I tell her something she already knows.

"Yeah, well, you can still glow, but you always have," she says, now putting it on a little thickly.

"Yes, she has. I'm proud to be her dad." I roll my eyes at the two of them. Especially him. I was afraid he wouldn't be proud after the stunt I pulled by lying to him about my suspicions of being pregnant. Instead, he tugged me into his arms like the protective father he is and bawled. He cried for my strength, happiness, and loyalty. Then, between those tears, he bitched me out like he used to when I was a teenager. Scolded me like he's never done before. As old as I am, there is nothing like standing there hearing the disappointment in your father's voice, yet at the same time knowing how proud he is. It's a paradox to a question I will never figure out unless the tables turn and it happens to me. Nevertheless, it won't happen again.

"Speaking of glowing." I look away from my dad to Alina, who looks absolutely stunning with her small bump, her tanned skin, and her pregnant glow in her bikini.

"I might be glowing, but it has nothing to do with being pregnant; it has everything to do with that." She points to all four men now standing in a row in the water, kids on top of their shoulders, Diesel standing in front of Cain, begging for Justice to get down. She won't do it. Not when the most important man in her life has a hold of her.

"I'm getting a picture." Deidre pulls her camera out of her bag, adjusts the baby, and moves stealthily through the sand.

My smile widens, my horizon is large, and my heart is filled.

ROAN

An entire month of pure fucking heaven and not a damn thing but the salty breeze and water for miles. No care in the world, no ringing of the phone. I haven't asked Ivan a thing about my empire since we've been down here. It's a fortress that awaits my return.

And now, with only a few days left, I hand my wailing son over to Alina, who needs to lay him down for his nap.

"Daddy has to go somewhere, buddy. He'll be back soon. Let's go read and cuddle with Mommy?" she says, places a sweet-tasting kiss on my lips that I want more of later, turns in her sexy little black bikini, and walks back toward our house with the rest of the family, Silas included.

I adjust my hard cock in my board shorts, pick up my bag, and hand it to Cain. His smile is tight, sad, and raw as he clutches it firmly in his hand.

"You guys ready?" Dilan hollers from the dock, where he waits inside of his speedboat that's more like a house. Cost well over a million dollars. The best investment he's made besides his wife. I doubt anyone of us would disagree with our choices of the women we fell in love with. I know I sure the fuck don't.

"Yeah. You better have that bar stocked with some Beam." Aidan scales up the steps to the dock, his bigass body blocking my view from the priceless face I know all too well he's receiving from Dilan. The man hates the taste of whiskey. Give that punk a cold beer of any kind, and he's happier than a kid on a tit. Well, I don't know about that, but the fucker is happy.

"Fuck no. I don't have any of that prissy shit on here. This is one of those bring-your-own-damn-whiskey parties." Aidan's face falls. I burst out laughing.

"Bullshit, motherfucker." He heads straight to the bar, opens up one of the cabinets, and I swear to Christ his moan sounds like he just came in his swim shorts.

"Dumb fuck," he hollers, snatches his bottle along with mine and Cain's, and lugs it to us.

"Take a seat, pussy," Dilan hollers from above, pushes this bad boy forward, and hits the high, open sea.

"Here's to Bronzer and Priscilla." Cain twists the cap off his bottle, takes a swig right from it, and then holds it up in the air. I do the same. It's not the time, nor the place to savor the sweet taste; it's the time to feel the burn. To feel the pain one last time for the lives that were taken too soon.

I tilt my head up to the blazing sun and allow my eyes to drift shut while I recollect the first few days after I made my last kill. The one after which I went back to my parents' house after driving around until daylight started to crest over the horizon. The one that finally put the pain I've carried around since I was a kid to rest. I showered down at the barn in the small, locker-room-style stalls my dad put in and burned my clothes, shoes, boxers, and anything else I had that reminded me of that motherfucker. When everyone else was finished, we made our way to the house, stripped out of our clean clothes, and I don't know about everyone else, but I slept for an entire day. Could have kept going too, except I heard my kid screaming for me. Exhaustion had worn me out. Drained me dry for longer than I can remember, and now it's fucking finally over. My life started fresh when I crawled out of bed with messy hair and nasty teeth, and took my boy outside to play. Two hours later, we went in to eat; he went down for a nap, and I went looking for Calla.

To say I didn't want to choke her when she told me she thought she was pregnant but went ahead with her job to help anyway is the highest understatement. I flew out of my chair, told her that would be the last time she will ever pull a stunt like that. I expected her to bitch, scream, and stand up to me. She did none of those things. She meekly said, "Okay, Roan. Whatever you say." "Damn right, it's whatever I say," I told her. That was it, end of the subject; no one has brought it up since and no one will. That's how it needs to be done. None of us should dwell on what ifs, or buts, or the whys of something that's already been done. She made her bed by keeping it from us; she can lie in it unmade, or she can get up, make her bed, and deal with her guilt on her own. I love her, respect her like no other. One thing I will not do is overprotect her from her mistake. She did what she did out of loyalty. I will make sure her loyalties lie elsewhere from now on.

The engine cuts on the boat, causing me to drift back from memories I'm going to work on forgetting after today. I need to be able to move forward, to expand this empire and to make my dad proud.

"This is a good spot, yeah?" Dilan asks then cracks open a beer.

"Yeah." Cain stands and places his half-empty pint on the table with all of us following suit. We trail behind him to the end of the boat and watch him pull out the gold-plated urn filled with our dear friends' ashes. It chokes me up to do this. There isn't a day gone by I wouldn't give to have them here with us right now.

"I'm not a man of words for shit like this," Cain stutters through his tears as he starts to twist off the cap.

"Let them go, brother." And so he does. On a day when I finally found my resurrection.

Which is, at times the most important people in your life can be taken away, but it's your memories of them which remind you of who you are.

I'm Roan Diamond, and this is my EMPIRE.

The End

Acknowledgements

There are times when you have one person who puts an entire thought out process into perspective with very few words. I'm lucky enough to have that person. The one who points out mistakes and errors with nothing but my best interest in mind. To help make me shine.

This series boosted my confidence. It proved to me that I can do it. That I can live the dream and with each book I write I'm improving. None of this would be possible without my friend and editor Julia Goda. This incredible lady has brought me to new hopes, new dreams. I owe her for helping make this series what it is. Her ability to see things that I could not. To make every one of these books shine. Julia, I cannot thank you enough for taking me on during a time when I was freaking out. Panicking in a way that had me pulling my hair out. Your skills impress me. Your kind word spur to action the quick witted side of my brain. I will never be able to thank you enough for being on my side. I simply adore you!

CP Smith. You, my sweet friend, have the patience of a saint. Poor woman has me bugging her about formatting and downloading with every book. You're stuck with me my sweet girl.

Karrie Mellott Puskas. My love, my bestie, my co-blogger. I have a sister in you. One that I admire and respect. Our talks loosen me up when I need it. They make me realize what a true friend I have in you. I always have your back, girl.

I could write an entire book back here thanking people who have helped me on the journey of writing this series. If you read, shared, commented, left a review, or bought this series you have helped in more ways than you will know. Without any one person I would not be doing what I love. I love my job but, it's not always about the writing. It's about meeting people. Making friends and talking. My days are filled with chatting away about nothing and everything. I thank you all for that and toss a big internet hug to each one of you.

God bless you all for taking a chance on me!
Until next time
Kathy

Other Books By Kathy Coopmans

The Shelter Me Series
Shelter Me
Rescue Me
Keep Me

The Contrite Duet
Contrite
Reprisal

The Syndicate Series
The Warth of Cain
The Redeption of Roan
The Absolution of Aidan
The Deliverance of Dilan

The Elite Forces Series
Ice
Fire
<u>Stone</u>

Made in the USA
Charleston, SC
10 September 2016